Silhouette®

1514
January

Man Behind the Badge

PAMELA TOTH

WINCHESTER
BRIDES

SPECIAL EDITION™

#1 *New York Times* bestselling author

NORA ROBERTS

**presents the passionate
heart of the city that
never sleeps.**

TRULY Madly MANHATTAN

containing

LOCAL HERO
and
DUAL IMAGE

And coming in May
**ENGAGING
THE ENEMY**

containing

A WILL AND A WAY
and
BOUNDARY LINES

*Available at your favorite
retail outlet.*

Silhouette®

Where love comes alive™

ISBN 0-373-24514-9

9 780373 245147

5 0 4 7 5

EAN

"I'm Charlie Winchester, your local sheriff,"

he said, touching two fingers to the brim of his hat. He flashed a smile that revealed straight white teeth and twin dimples. His dark eyes studied her with leisurely thoroughness from behind amber lenses.

"I'll bet you're the new vet."

"How'd you guess?" Robin asked.

He folded his tanned, muscular arms across his chest. "It wasn't a guess. You've got out-of-state plates and a rental trailer."

"Pretty clever of you," she replied dryly, taking a step back from all that hunky broad-shouldered masculinity before it gave her the vapors.

From inside the clinic, a phone rang and a dog barked.

"I gotta go," she said, turning.

"My office is right down the street, if you need anything."

She waved but didn't look back. "Yeah, thanks. See you."

Charlie stroked his chin thoughtfully as he watched her disappear. "Count on it, sweetheart."

Dear Reader,

Our resolution is to start the year with a bang in Silhouette Special Edition! And so we are featuring Peggy Webb's *The Accidental Princess*—our pick for this month's READERS' RING title. You'll want to use the riches in this romance to facilitate discussions with your friends and family! In this lively tale, a plain Jane agrees to be the local Dairy Princess and wins the heart of the bad-boy reporter who wants her story…among other things.

Next up, Sherryl Woods thrills her readers once again with the newest installment of THE DEVANEYS—*Michael's Discovery.* Follow this ex-navy SEAL hero as he struggles to heal from battle—and save himself from falling hard for his beautiful physical therapist! Pamela Toth's *Man Behind the Badge,* the third book in her popular WINCHESTER BRIDES miniseries, brings us another stunning hero in the form of a flirtatious sheriff, whose wild ways are numbered when he meets—and wants to rescue—a sweet, yet reclusive woman with a secret past. Talking about secrets, a doctor hero is stunned when he finds a baby— maybe even *his* baby—on the doorstep in Victoria Pade's *Maybe My Baby,* the second book in her BABY TIMES THREE miniseries. Add a feisty heroine to the mix, and you have an instant family.

Teresa Southwick delivers an unforgettable story in *Midnight, Moonlight & Miracles.* In it, a nurse feels a strong attraction to her handsome patient, yet she doesn't want him to discover the *real* connection between them. And Patricia Kay's *Annie and the Confirmed Bachelor* explores the blossoming love between a self-made millionaire and a woman who can't remember her past. Can their romance survive?

This month's lineup is packed with intrigue, passion, complex heroines and heroes who never give up. Keep your own resolution to live life romantically, with a treat from Silhouette Special Edition. Happy New Year, and happy reading!

Karen Taylor Richman
Senior Editor

Please address questions and book requests to:
Silhouette Reader Service
U.S.: 3010 Walden Ave., P.O. Box 1325, Buffalo, NY 14269
Canadian: P.O. Box 609, Fort Erie, Ont. L2A 5X3

Man Behind the Badge

PAMELA TOTH

SPECIAL EDITION™

Published by Silhouette Books

America's Publisher of Contemporary Romance

Dedicated with appreciation and affection to my editor,
Karen Taylor Richman, for her support,
her understanding and—most of all—her patience,
above and beyond the call of duty.

 SILHOUETTE BOOKS

ISBN 0-373-24514-9

MAN BEHIND THE BADGE

Copyright © 2003 by Pamela Toth

Visit Silhouette at www.eHarlequin.com

Printed in U.S.A.

Books by Pamela Toth

Silhouette Special Edition

Thunderstruck #411
Dark Angel #515
Old Enough To Know Better #624
Two Sets of Footprints #729
A Warming Trend #760
Walk Away, Joe #850
The Wedding Knot #905
Rocky Mountain Rancher #951
Buchanan's Bride #1012
Buchanan's Baby #1017
Buchanan's Return #1096
The Paternity Test #1138
†*The Mail-Order Mix-Up* #1197
Buchanan's Pride #1239
The Baby Legacy #1299
Millionaire Takes a Bride #1353
†*Cattleman's Honor* #1502
†*Man Behind the Badge* #1514

Silhouette Romance

Kissing Games #500
The Ladybug Lady #595

*Buckles & Broncos
†The Winchester Brides

PAMELA TOTH

USA TODAY bestselling author Pamela Toth was born in Wisconsin, but grew up in Seattle where she attended the University of Washington and majored in art. Now living on the Puget Sound area's east side, she has two daughters, Erika and Melody, and two Siamese cats.

Recently she took a lead from one of her romances and married her high school sweetheart, Frank. They live in a town house within walking distance of a bookstore and an ice-cream shop, two of life's necessities, with a fabulous view of Mount Rainier. When she's not writing, she enjoys traveling with her husband, reading, playing FreeCell on the computer, doing counted cross-stitch and researching new story ideas. She's been an active member of Romance Writers of America since 1982.

Her books have won several awards and they claim regular spots on the Waldenbooks bestselling romance list. She loves hearing from readers and can be reached at P.O. Box 5845, Bellevue, WA 98006. For a personal reply, a SASE is appreciated.

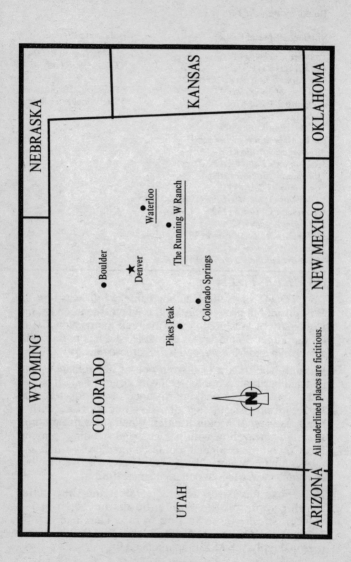

WYOMING

NEBRASKA

COLORADO

UTAH

• Boulder

★ Denver

Pikes Peak •

• Colorado Springs

• Waterloo

The Running W Ranch

N

KANSAS

ARIZONA   NEW MEXICO   OKLAHOMA

All underlined places are fictititious.

Chapter One

With a sigh of relief, Robin Marlowe pulled up in front of a small box-shaped building at the outskirts of town and parked next to a dusty SUV with a dent in the side. The soda she'd gulped down when she stopped for gas at a truck stop back in Kansas was starting to make her squirm on the hot vinyl seat of her aging tan VW Rabbit. Her fingers were cramped around the wheel.

The faded sign beside the front door said Dr. Elliot Harmon, D.V.M. Specialty—Large Animals.

Dr. Harmon's large-animal practice was the very reason Robin had traded the familiar crowds and chaos of Chicago for the empty Colorado plains, eerily silent but for the sound of the wind. She'd come to Waterloo in order to gain experience treating horses and cattle. She was looking forward to meeting her new boss almost as much as finding a rest room— if he hadn't given up on her and hired someone else.

If he had, maybe he'd let her use the facilities anyway.

Robin blamed her delayed arrival on a broken water pump that had wrecked her budget as well as her schedule. According to the mechanic, whose rates were higher than her dentist's back home, pulling the fully loaded utility trailer through the late-August heat had overtaxed her car's small engine.

She probably should have called Doc Harmon to explain, but she'd figured it would be harder for him to fire her in person. Now she wasn't so sure.

Robin had managed to extract herself from the sticky car seat without losing any skin from the backs of her thighs and was smoothing the wrinkles from her navy-blue skirt when the door of the clinic burst open.

"Dr. Marlowe?" demanded the elderly man hurrying toward her, a black leather bag gripped in one bony hand. Tall and lean as a coatrack, he was slightly stooped, his shock of white hair combed back from a thin face with a high forehead and a beaky nose. He was wearing a plaid sport shirt with sleeves that fluttered in the faint breeze and tan slacks that hung on his spare frame like cheap slipcovers.

"Yes, that's me." Robin removed her sunglasses

and shielded her eyes against bright sunlight, bracing herself for bad news. "You must be—"

"Doc Harmon." He gave her hand a quick, hard squeeze. "Glad to see you. I expected you yesterday, but no matter. I've got an emergency and my receptionist is out sick." He gestured at the building behind him. "Can you man the phone till I get back?"

"Uh, I guess." Her stomach fluttered with a mix of apprehension and relief. What if she messed up?

"Just take a message," he said, heading for the SUV. "Tell 'em I'm out to Winchesters' spread." Without waiting for a reply, he opened the door and climbed in with surprising agility for someone his age.

Robin's hand tightened on the shoulder strap of her purse as she watched him start the engine and lower the window. Perhaps he was too shorthanded to fire her just yet, but he still might.

"I'm sorry I'm late," she said, raising her voice. "My car—"

"You're here now." He barely spared her a glance as he backed up. "My cell phone number's on the counter."

Slightly dazed, Robin watched him drive away. She was hot, thirsty and nearly broke. She needed a bathroom, a place to stay and, thanks to the gold-plated water pump, an advance on her pay.

"Not much of a welcome, huh?"

The unexpected touch on her shoulder and the male voice at her ear startled a shriek out of her. She spun around to see a man wearing a shiny silver starred pinned to his khaki uniform shirt.

"I'm sorry. I didn't mean to scare you." He flashed a smile that revealed straight white teeth and twin dimples. Only a nose that looked as if it must have been broken saved him from being entirely too handsome. "I'm Charlie Winchester, your local sheriff," he added, touching two fingers to the brim of his hat.

"Uh, hi," Robin managed, still a little shaken. Her nerves had been stretched tight during the long drive from Chicago, and her shoulders ached from hunching over the steering wheel since she'd left the shabby motel early this morning.

But wasn't Winchester the name Doc Harmon had mentioned when he'd told her where he was headed? Did they own the town? She could hardly ask the sheriff, whose dark eyes studied her with leisurely thoroughness from behind amber lenses.

Robin knew what he'd see, a plain woman with black hair cut ruthlessly short and a face free of anything fancier than road dust. She wasn't a girly girl, and she didn't bother much with paints and perfumes. It irked her that she had to tip her head back in order to look at his face instead of his wide chest. She was small but wiry, and as her aunt Dot used to say, Robin was tall on the inside, where it counted.

Robin wasn't so sure of that anymore, and her aunt was no longer around to ask.

"I'll bet you're the new vet," the sheriff said as if he was prompting her to speak.

Robin's tongue came unstuck, and she peeled it off the roof of her mouth. "How'd you guess?"

He folded his tanned, muscular arms across his chest. His hands, she noticed, were ringless. "It wasn't a guess." He feigned a hurt expression. "I get paid to know things. That's why I'm the sheriff. Besides, you've got out-of-state plates, a rental trailer in tow and the doc expected you yesterday."

"Pretty clever of you," she replied dryly, taking a step back from all that hunky broad-shouldered masculinity before it gave her the vapors. Good manners kicked in, courtesy of her late aunt. "My name's Robin Marlowe."

His grin widened. "See, I was right. Reading clues is part of my job, that and chasing bad guys. There aren't a lot of those in Waterloo, so I have time to greet newcomers, too."

"Kind of like a welcoming committee packing heat," she drawled, her gaze flicking to the imposing holster on his hip.

His eyes widened, but his laugh came easy. "Yes, ma'am, I guess you could say that."

From inside the clinic, a phone started ringing and a dog began to bark.

"Oh, nuts," she muttered, turning. "I gotta go." She didn't mind the interruption, but instead of ogling Sheriff Tex she should have been looking for the bathroom while she'd had the chance.

"Nice to meet you," she called automatically over her shoulder as she hurried up the front steps.

"You, too, Doc Marlowe," the sheriff replied. "My office is right down the street, if you need anything. It's the one with the bars on the windows."

She waved, but didn't look back. "Yeah, thanks. See you."

Charlie Winchester stroked his chin thoughtfully as he watched her disappear.

"Count on it, sweetheart," he murmured. For such a little thing, she had legs like a colt—long and fine-boned. And lips a man could settle into like a feather-bed, if they were anywhere near as lush as they looked.

Welcoming committee, huh? Checking out the new arrivals was part of his job, even the ones who weren't cute as pixies and reportedly single like this new little gal. He'd better talk to her again, though, just to make sure she wasn't really an escaped con or an illegal, impersonating the vet's new helper in order to commit some nefarious crime in Charlie's town.

He hadn't meant to scare her when he'd touched her shoulder, but she'd gone as stiff as a calf stuck in a blizzard. The sight of his badge hadn't seemed to relax her a bit. Her big brown eyes had stayed wary, without a spark of female awareness to warm them, and her mouth hadn't softened. Despite the gun at Charlie's hip, most women saw right away that he was no more threat than a six-foot teddy bear.

From eight months to eighty, he liked women, always had, and they usually liked him right back. Robin hadn't seemed overly impressed, though, not even by his uniform, tailored and pressed at the local laundry, or his badge. It was something a couple of the local ladies still gushed over, as though they were picturing him wearing the star and not much else. Made a man darned uncomfortable, being looked at like that.

Robin Marlowe had captured his interest. No, his ''professional concern,'' he corrected himself, even though it was doubtful that Doc Harmon would hire an assistant with outstanding warrants or felonious intentions—even one compact enough for Charlie to easily scoop up and cuddle or whose short haircut exposed earlobes begging to be nibbled.

He hitched up his belt and eyed the clinic. The ringing of the phone had stopped while he stood in the street like a lovesick calf, but the dog's rhythmic barking kept time with the sound of the new vet's voice through the open doorway. It had a husky quality that hinted at smoky, dimly lit bars and honky-tonk women.

Curiously Charlie circled her car, a nondescript tan Rabbit with barely legal tires, Illinois plates and a utility trailer hitched behind it. On the back seat of the car rested a hard-sided suitcase like you'd find in a thrift shop, and several cardboard cartons. One was open and held books, probably veterinary tomes. The other boxes were taped shut. Behind the front seat was a pair of high rubber boots that looked new, an electric fan that didn't, a coffeemaker and a cheap toaster, cords all neatly coiled. On the front passenger seat were an empty water bottle, two candy wrappers and a Colorado road map that had been refolded incorrectly. Some kind of crystal dangled from the rearview mirror, its faceted surfaces sparkling in the sunlight.

Charlie debated whether to go inside and ask her a few more questions, maybe see if she'd be interested in dinner or help in finding a place to stay, but the cell phone clipped to his belt chose that moment to claim his attention. Filing away his first impressions of Waterloo's newest resident, he checked to see if a crime wave had just hit town.

Robin had been watching Sheriff Winchester through the front window of the clinic as she tried to explain to a suspicious-sounding older woman why *she* was answering Doc Harmon's phone and not his "regular girl."

"I don't know where Erline is today," Robin said for the third time, explaining again who *she* was and what had happened to the real vet. The term hadn't exactly endeared the caller to Robin, but she resisted the urge to tell the old bat she had duct-taped the "real vet" and stuffed him in the supply closet just so she could have the thrill of this phone call. Curbing her tongue wasn't easy, especially when the pressure in her bladder increased with each word.

By the time she'd taken a message and glanced outside, the sheriff had disappeared. After she'd found the bathroom and made use of it with a groan of relief, she did a bit of exploring.

The clinic was small but complete. In addition to the reception area, there were two examining rooms, a well-equipped surgery, a small lab and a supply room. Its only current occupant was the dog, a black lab mix with a bandaged leg, sitting in a roomy crate. When he saw Robin, his tail wagged, but he stopped barking and began whining instead. He wiggled so hard the cage shook. After she'd made sure he had water, she let him lick her fingers and she scratched his chin while he squeezed his dark eyes shut in obvious pleasure.

Typical male, she thought with a grin. Noisy and easy to satisfy.

As if *she* knew anything about satisfying a male, or wanted to. Her grin faded as fast as it had appeared.

Despite her fatigue, she was eager to get settled and start working. Doc Harmon had promised to find her a rental she could afford, but she didn't have an address, and of course she couldn't leave until he got back. There wasn't anything she could really do here until he showed her around, and she was hesitant to poke through his files, so she went back to the reception area and sat down at the big desk. There was a phone with two lines, thankfully silent, but no computer, which didn't surprise her. With a sigh she started flipping idly through the open appointment book. Nothing scheduled until late afternoon and no telling how long Erline would be out sick, so she might as well get familiar with the setup.

Charlie didn't need to follow the faint track through the grass to find the pasture where the two owners of the Running W had said they'd meet him. The land was as familiar as the face he saw in the mirror, and the men nearly so. He'd spent his youth on the Running W, chasing after his older brothers, Adam and Travis, and working beside them.

Topping a rise, Charlie spotted them standing with the vet near their rigs and several mounds that appeared to be sleeping cattle.

A chill went through Charlie. His hands tightened on the wheel of his Jeep as he struggled to replace a rancher's sick dismay with the objectivity of a lawman.

No one had been more surprised than Charlie when he'd beaten out a bully and a green kid to win the election ten months before, and not everyone was happy about it, considering his reputation as a skirt-chasing lightweight who'd been riding along on his brothers' coattails. He'd discovered a knack for the job, equal parts politician, paper pusher and crime solver, but he knew convincing his detractors would take time.

Whether chasing a woman or a criminal, Charlie was a patient man.

"Hey, bro, thanks for coming out," Adam said after he'd parked next to the ranch pickup and joined the other three men.

"No problem." Briefly, Charlie clasped the hand Adam extended. Charlie had sold out his share of the ranch to his brothers, but they'd all remained close. Today's summons was no surprise; Charlie would have been upset if they hadn't called.

"How you doing?" he asked Travis, whose grim expression matched Adam's.

"I've been better," Travis replied around the stalk of grass stuck in the corner of his mouth. "Dead cattle's a bad business."

"That's for sure. What happened?" Charlie looked from him to the vet, who'd been bent over a dun-colored steer with his black leather bag open beside him. Five other carcasses were scattered nearby.

The old vet packed up the specimens he'd been collecting. "I'll know for sure when we hear back from the lab," he said by way of greeting as he got to his feet, "but it looks pretty obvious to me what happened."

The sick feeling Charlie had been trying to blot out came flooding back. "What do you mean?" he asked.

Doc Harmon glanced at Adam. "Show him what you found."

Adam held up a bag Charlie hadn't noticed before. "This was mixed in with some feed we found scattered nearby."

Charlie glanced at the printing on the bag. It was

a common brand. "Have any idea how it got out here?" he asked.

A muscle flexed along Adam's jaw as he shook his head. "It's the same kind we keep in the shed," he replied. "I'll have to check and see if it came from there, but everyone who works here knows better than to leave rat poison anywhere near the stock."

The vet cleared his throat. When Charlie glanced at him, he said, "Looks deliberate to me. Maybe you'd better ask your brothers if they've made any enemies lately."

When she heard a vehicle pull up outside, Robin set aside the three-month-old magazine she'd been reading and went to the window. Once in a while a car went by and she'd had several calls; no one had come into the clinic. Even the dog in the back was asleep.

She recognized the SUV, relieved Doc Harmon had returned. She had a lot of questions, a couple of them being whether she had anywhere to sleep tonight—or a job tomorrow. As she continued to watch through the window, he got out of his car, grabbed his bag and walked over to the olive-green Cherokee that had pulled in behind him. It had a gold star painted on the door and an official-looking row of lights on top. Through the back window she could see a rifle rack, and it wasn't empty.

Robin couldn't hear what they were saying and the vet's back was to her as he leaned forward, but the

smile Sheriff Winchester had worn earlier was no-
ticeably absent. After a couple more moments, Doc
Harmon straightened up.

The sheriff glanced at the clinic window and Robin
moved away so he wouldn't see her spying on them
and get the wrong idea. By the time her boss came
through the front door, she was standing behind the
counter trying to look indispensable.

"Everything okay?" she asked innocently as the
dog in the back room began barking again.

"Some days I really dislike this job." He set his
bag on the counter, looking tired. "How did you get
on? Any emergencies?"

Robin told him about a couple of the calls she'd
taken. "Nothing urgent," she concluded. "I told
them Erline would get back to them. Do you know
when she'll be in?"

"Tomorrow, I hope. Thanks for covering."

"It doesn't sound like things went well at the
Winchesters' spread," she asked, prompted by both
professional interest and personal curiosity. She'd
mentally reviewed her brief encounter with the sheriff
several times, wondering if her abrupt dash into the
clinic had made her seem unfriendly, and then telling
herself it didn't matter what he thought as long as it
didn't affect her professionally.

The vet picked up his messages, but she had the
impression that he wasn't really looking at them.
"Half a dozen dead cattle at the biggest ranch in these

parts,'' he said finally. ''One of the hands found them this morning.''

Robin could understand his reaction. This was cattle country. A contagious disease could endanger an entire herd if it wasn't treated in time. No wonder he looked worried. ''Were you able to make a diagnosis?'' she asked.

He ran his hand through his hair, making it stand on end. ''It looks like someone tainted their feed with rodent poison. The sheriff is looking into it.''

''The sheriff?'' Robin echoed.

Doc Harmon nodded. ''Cattle will eat damn near anything. Ranchers don't leave poison around for them to get into.''

''So it was deliberate?'' Robin asked. ''Why would anyone do that?''

He shrugged. ''Everyone has enemies.''

''Is there some kind of range war going on around here?'' she probed.

His smile was fleeting. ''This isn't the Old West, my girl, but bad things still happen. Could be an unhappy ex-employee or an envious neighbor. Those boys have worked hard, and they've done well. I even heard a rumor that they'd had an offer for their land.''

He glanced around the office. ''Did you get a chance to explore?''

Robin would have liked to ask more about the Winchesters, but she didn't want to push. ''A little.'' She clasped her hands together and took a deep breath. ''I know you expected me to get here yesterday, but I had car trouble. I should have let you know.'' Before she could add anything more, anxiety closed around her throat like a noose, choking off her voice.

All Doc Harmon did was shrug again. ''I was out most of the day and we've been having trouble with the answering machine, anyway. It's nice you were here to get the phone today, though, so no one started thinking I'd died or retired.''

He glanced out the window as she nearly went limp with relief. ''Car running okay now? You'll need something reliable, you know.''

Her gaze followed his to where the sorry little coupe sat baking in the sun. ''Oh, yes, it's fine,'' she assured him. ''I guess I just expected too much, towing a trailer full of all my worldly goods.''

The doc glanced at the messages again and then he set them on the counter. ''Speaking of which, I rented you a little house at the edge of town. If the bar down the street from it is too noisy, you can look for something else, but there's not much of a choice right in town.''

Especially in my price range, she added silently. ''I'm sure it will be fine. Thank you for going to the trouble.'' She was trying to figure out how she could possibly ask for an advance when he pulled open a drawer in the battered desk.

''No trouble. Figured you might need to get a few things.'' He thrust a check at her.

Robin stared speechlessly at the amount. She'd

been on her own for so long, counting on no one but herself, that she was blindsided by his gesture. She ducked her head, her eyes filling with tears that she barely managed to blink away before they ran down her cheeks. She had to be more tired than she'd realized to get so emotional.

"Thank you." She looked up. "I can use this."

The crusty expression relaxed for a moment. "You'll earn it," he said gruffly. "I'm an ogre to work for. Ask anyone."

Somehow she doubted that very much. For one of the few times she could remember since her aunt had died, the hard knot of tension in Robin's chest eased up. When she'd been sending out résumés, she'd almost decided not to answer his ad, figuring an old geezer in a small town surrounded by cattle ranches would never consider hiring a woman as his assistant. "You don't scare me," she replied somberly.

"We'll see about that." Chuckling, he glanced at the plain round wall clock above the door. "I can manage for now. Why don't you take the rest of the afternoon to get settled? Open a bank account, get some groceries. I've got the key to your place here somewhere." He fished around in the drawer while Robin folded the check he'd given her and tucked it into her pocket.

"Are you sure? I can stay, if you need me."

He handed her a brass key. "The lights and water are hooked up, and I had your phone connected."

"What do I owe you?" she asked. "Didn't you have to pay deposits on the utilities?"

This time his laugh was more of a cackle. "This ain't Chicago, Doctor. All I did was to tell them you were coming to work for me. And this way, people can start calling *you* in the middle of the night 'stead of me when their prize stud gets a sliver in his arse."

She wondered how long it would be before anyone around here actually did request her services, rather than merely tolerate her whenever the "real" vet was otherwise occupied. "Can you give me directions to my house?" she asked after she'd thanked him again.

The words *my house* danced on Robin's tongue. Since moving out of Aunt Dot's, she'd lived in college dorms and rundown apartments with an assortment of roommates to keep the rent low, but she'd never had a place to really call her own. She was determined to make this a real home, despite it being another rental and no matter what the condition.

"I'll draw you a map." He grabbed a scratch pad. "It's not hard to find. Nothing in this town is, but you'll get lost a few times heading out on calls, so you'll need this, too." He handed her a cell phone. "You pay for your personal calls."

She swallowed. "I don't have anyone to call."

His eyes narrowed. "No family?"

"My aunt died while I was in college." She braced herself for more questions, but he didn't ask them. Despite all the help he'd given her, she was an employee and that was all, she reminded herself. Her life story wouldn't interest him.

Except for that one time at veterinary school, which she made a point never to think about, her life was pretty darned boring. Just the way she liked it.

He drew three intersecting lines on the paper and made two X's. "You're here," he said, pointing an one X with the pencil. "Go five blocks to Aspen and take a right. Turn left on the next street, Nugget, and look for a little house painted yellow, number 505. Can't miss it."

Robin started to thank him again. "Dr. Harmon—"

"Call me that, people will get me mixed up with the medic, Dr. Nash. I'm just plain old Doc." He cocked his head to the side, considering. "Don't suppose I can call you Birdy. Kind of a clever nickname, don't you think?"

"No," she replied firmly. "No way."

He shrugged. "Didn't think so. Okay, you scat, before something comes up. See you in the morning, at eight sharp. You got my number if you need anything before then."

Robin hesitated, but the phone rang and he reached for it. She waited to see if he'd want her to stay, after all, but he waved her off before turning his back.

She didn't need to be told twice, so she hurried out the door before he could change his mind. To her relief, her car started right away. As she drove down the street, following his crude map, she tried not to get her hopes up about the house. It was probably a dump.

When she passed the sheriff's office, she kept her head turned straight, not wanting to be caught looking for him. He wasn't for her, she reminded herself. No man was.

Chapter Two

"Hi, sweetheart. How 'bout bringing me a steak sandwich and a longneck?" Charlie gave the waitress a quick smile as he settled himself onto a bar stool.

"Sure, boss. As long as you're off duty," she replied in a throaty voice. "I wouldn't want to break the law."

He patted his shirt pocket. "I'm not wearing my badge, Rita. You won't get in any trouble." With her black hair and dark, liquid eyes, Rita was an attractive woman—especially when she sucked in her breath so her generous curves strained against the fabric of her low-cut knit top as she was doing now.

If he didn't have a rule against dating his employees, Charlie might have taken a run at her. When he pursued a woman, he didn't want to wonder if she was genuinely attracted to him or just worried about keeping her job, especially a single mother like Rita.

"Fries with that or salad?" she asked, tossing back her hair to give him an enticing view of her throat.

He grinned his appreciation of her assets. "How about both, with ranch on the side?"

"Sure thing. Be right back."

After she'd gotten his beer, sent him a last regretful glance from beneath a fringe of thick lashes and swaggered off to give his sandwich order to the cook, Charlie glanced around the room. There were people sitting at three tables and two men in hard hats at the other end of the bar watching soccer on the overhead television. Not bad for a weekday, especially this early in the evening.

"You singing tonight, Sheriff?" called out an older woman seated with her husband.

"'Fraid not, Maxine." He touched two fingers to the brim of his Stetson. "My second job's keeping me hopping, but I'll be here on Friday. Maybe you can get Fred to bring you back then."

She looked over her shoulder at her husband. "That's my birthday. We'll be here."

Charlie toasted her with his beer bottle. "And I'll be singing just for you, darlin'."

She laughed, but her cheeks turned pink. "I'll hold you to it." Her husband leaned forward to whisper in her ear, and Charlie swiveled back around as Rita brought his salad. From ranching to the restaurant business and part-time lounge singer to law enforcement. Life was a hell of a ride.

"How are the boys?" he asked Rita.

She set down his silverware and dish of ranch dressing. "They're crazy about the toy trucks you gave them. Thanks, honey."

"No problem." He knew her ex rarely sent money, and his nephews had more toys than they could ever use. When he'd mentioned the waitress to Rory and Emily, his brothers' wives, their youngest kids had gone through their toy chests.

"You bat those pretty eyes at the guys sitting at the other end of the bar, should double your tips," he suggested to Rita.

The touch of her hand on his shoulder was fleeting, her voice soft in his ear. "Enjoy your salad."

A few moments later, after she'd brought the rest of his meal and he'd devoured half the sandwich while he'd mulled over his workday, a burst of laughter distracted him. Rita had followed his suggestion and was talking to the construction workers.

She'd be okay. This was a respectable bar, and she knew how to take care of herself.

Charlie turned back to his food, but eating alone had lost its appeal. Everyone in town knew him, and he knew most of them. His older brothers were his closest friends. He liked their wives, adored their children and was welcome anytime. It was a welcome he was careful not to wear out.

The sound of Rita's laughter reminded him of the

woman he'd met earlier, Robin Marlowe, even though the two appeared to be polar opposites. If Dr. Marlowe had found him attractive, she'd hidden it well. If she hadn't rushed off, he might have invited her to dinner just to see her reaction.

Maybe he'd have to buy himself a dog, one that would need vaccinations at the local clinic.

Robin was unpacking the last of her aunt's dishes and putting them into the kitchen cupboard when a knock at the back door nearly caused her to drop a dinner plate adorned with fat pink roses. She set it carefully down on the counter and ran a hand through her short hair. She'd only met two people so far, her boss and the sheriff. This was a small town, not Chicago, so perhaps one of them had come by to check on her.

Nerves fluttered in her chest. She was almost relieved when she peeked through the window and saw an elderly couple standing on the side porch. They looked harmless.

Robin flipped the lock and opened the door. The woman, a little bird of a thing with fluffy white hair and wire-rimmed glasses, was holding a pie with a flaky, golden crust. The man behind her wore coveralls and a Broncos baseball cap. His scraggly gray hair needed trimming.

"I'm Mae Simms and this is my husband, Ed," the woman said quickly. "We don't mean to intrude, but we wanted to say hello and to give you this." She thrust the pie into Robin's hands. "Welcome to Waterloo."

Her offering smelled fantastic. As Robin's stomach growled softly, she realized that she hadn't eaten in hours.

"Thank you," she said. Would they think her unfriendly if she didn't invite them in? She had so much to do, and she was tired. "I'm Robin. I was just unpacking."

"Oh, we know who you are, honey," the woman replied. "We live right next door in the blue house. You're renting this place from us."

"Ah." Robin wasn't sure what else to say. Their visit was the type of gesture her aunt would have made under similar circumstances. The thought warmed her. Balancing the pie, she nudged the door open wider with her elbow. "Would you like to come in? I've already unpacked my coffeemaker and some mugs. I'm sure I could find the coffee."

"Oh, no, dear." Mae was already backing away. She nudged Ed, who hadn't said a word. "You have things to do, I'm sure, and we're going for our walk." Reaching into the pocket of the purple nylon jacket she wore with matching pants, she pulled out a folded paper.

"Here's our phone number, just in case." She set it lightly on top of the pie. "If there's anything you need, give us a call."

Robin raised up the pan she was holding. The bottom was still warm. "Thank you again. I can't wait to sample this."

"She's won lots of ribbons at the fair." Ed's voice sounded rusty, as though he didn't use it much. "They cover most of one wall in the dining room."

"Never mind that," Mae scolded as she herded him off the porch like a border collie with a not-too-bright sheep. "Bye, now," she called back over her shoulder.

"Bye." Robin glanced past them at the neat blue house next door, separated from hers by a freshly painted white picket fence. The lots on this street were big, so the older, mostly small houses weren't jammed close together.

After her visitors had walked down the driveway, hand in hand, she set the pie on the table that had come with the rental and relocked the door. She'd have to see about a dead bolt. It would make her feel more secure.

Mouth watering, she rustled around until she found a fork. When she cut through the flaky crust, peach filling oozed up like liquid gold. She ate the first serving right from the pan.

With her hunger blunted, she fixed herself a cup of tea. While the water heated, she cut another generous slice of pie and set it on a plate. She'd be having it again for breakfast if she didn't get to the grocery store tonight. She should have asked Mae where it was, but the town only had one main street, so she doubted she'd get lost.

While the tea brewed, Robin looked around her with a sigh of satisfaction. The house was small, the furniture as outdated as the walnut cabinets and dark green counter, but it was clean and cozy. She would add her own touches: candles, knickknacks, pictures for the walls and pretty kitchen towels to replace the faded ones she'd brought with her.

The teddy bear cookie jar sitting on the counter caught her eye, and she blinked back sudden tears. That, the dishes and a few other keepsakes were all she had from Aunt Dot. Robin's cousin and his wife had kept everything else.

She lifted the mug of hot tea to her lips and was about to take a sip when she heard footsteps on the porch. The figure of a man appeared in the glass of the back door. Fear shot through Robin and then she recognized the sheriff. With a jerky movement that slopped hot tea onto her fingers, she set down the mug and got to her feet. She hoped he wasn't going to make a habit of startling her.

Apparently, no one used the front porch. If she wanted any privacy, she'd have to cover the window in the side door. The sheriff peered through it as she crossed the kitchen.

"Is there a problem, Sheriff?" she asked as she opened the door, wondering belatedly whether her face was smudged with newsprint from unwrapping her dishes. Funny, she hadn't thought of that when the older couple had come by.

In the confines of the covered porch, the sheriff

seemed bigger and bulkier than he'd appeared on the open street. The brim of his hat shadowed his expression. "It's only a problem if that's your car parked in the driveway," he replied with a serious expression.

"You know it is," she snapped. "You saw it earlier. Sorry I haven't had a chance to change the plates. How long do I have?"

He looked at the car and then back at her. "I'm not here about the plates. I was driving by, and I noticed that the tire is flat."

"Oh, no!" She tried to push past him, but he was as solid as a mountain and nearly as immovable.

"Whoa, there." Lightly he caught her shoulders. "Don't panic. I can change it for you."

She caught a whiff of masculine cologne before she twisted away from his touch. "That's not necessary. I can take care of myself." Realizing how shrill and ungrateful she must sound, she dragged in a steadying breath and met his puzzled gaze. "Thank you for your offer," she said more quietly, "and for stopping to tell me about it, but I can manage on my own."

Damn, but she hoped the spare hadn't gone flat. The last thing she wanted was for the sheriff to notice if it had and to think her incompetent. No, the *last* thing she wanted was for him to do her a favor and for her to *owe* him.

"Are you sure?" His dark eyes studied her for a moment, and then he glanced past her into the kitchen where a pile of partially unpacked boxes sat on the floor. "Looks like you've got enough to do right here. I wouldn't mistake you for a helpless female, not this one time."

Feeling embarrassed and invaded, Robin shifted her body in a futile attempt to block his view. He was tall enough to look over the top of her head if he'd wanted to, but he must have noticed her gesture and interpreted it correctly, because he half turned so he was looking out at the street.

His profile, despite the broken nose, was perfectly chiseled. Not that she noticed.

"I'm fine." Ignoring his jab, she gripped the edge of the door with one hand, ready to shut it. "Thanks again for stopping."

He glanced at her as though he was going to say something else, but her expression must have convinced him not to bother. He stepped off the porch instead.

"Okay, then," he said. "You take care."

Resisting the urge to watch him walk away, Robin shut the door resolutely. Then she sneaked into the living room, waiting for him to leave so she could deal with the tire. As she stood well back from the window, arms folded across her chest, he got back into the Cherokee and backed onto the street. Her breath stopped in her throat as he stared straight up at the spot where she stood. She was sure he couldn't see her through the lace curtains, but he raised two fingers to the brim of his hat in a mocking salute before he drove away.

Robin's arms tightened around her middle. She couldn't have been more irritated if he'd blown her a kiss. Why couldn't he be old and fat? If she intended to build a successful practice in Waterloo, she had to get along with people. Even if someone tried to make her feel embarrassed for standing in her own house and looking out her own window!

Before he drove to the corner, Charlie regretted his childish impulse. When he'd seen her figure backlit in the front window, he hadn't been able to resist letting her know he'd seen her. Especially after her lack of gratitude when he'd taken the trouble to stop and offer to change the tire.

His dented male ego urged him to forget about the prickly new vet. Either she wasn't interested or she liked playing hard to get, but either way, he didn't need the aggravation.

Charlie wasn't so conceited that he expected every woman in town to fall at his feet—even though more than a few of them had. Ever since grade school, he'd been popular with the opposite sex. Unfortunately, in the short time he'd been sheriff he'd come up against that same brittle shell Dr. Robin Marlowe wore on a couple of different occasions. Both of the other women had been victims in one way or another, one raped by a stranger and the other abused by her husband.

Charlie's fingers tightened on the wheel as he remembered the two women, one hardly more than a girl and the other looking older than she should. Bullies sickened him.

Robin aroused his curiosity, both professional and personal. Was she a victim, too, or was she just indifferent to the Winchester charm?

Either way, it was nice she had Mae Simms living right next door. Mae had been Charlie's teacher the year his mother ran off. He'd hurt too much to actually confide in her, but she'd gone out of her way to be kind to him and he'd never forgotten it. She and Ed would look out for their new neighbor, no matter how prickly Robin turned out to be.

Charlie sat at the four-way stop, trying to figure out the best way to approach Robin again. He was about to remove his foot from the brake pedal when a black Honda ran the stop sign on the cross street, nearly removing the front bumper on Charlie's Jeep. He got a quick glimpse of four boys in baseball caps as the car sped by, and he wondered how the hell they could have missed seeing his official vehicle with its rack of lights on top, as noticeable as an elephant wearing a diamond tiara.

Damn it. He was supposed to be off-duty. Slapping the steering wheel with the flat of his hand as he glanced both ways, Charlie hit the lights and siren. He rounded the corner and stomped on the gas in hot pursuit, laying a nice patch of rubber as he radioed his location to dispatch.

* * *

Robin had already walked outside to deal with her flat tire when she heard the police siren slice through the early evening peace like a cleaver through a cube of butter.

"Hotshot show-off," she muttered under her breath. No doubt Sheriff Winchester enjoyed flashing that tin star, throwing his weight around and playing with guns.

The last thought made her shiver. She didn't like guns. They made her nervous. She'd grown up in Chicago and she respected the police, but Sheriff Tex was almost too handsome, with matching dimples and an ah-shucks drawl meant to melt women like overheated candle wax.

Good thing Robin was immune to that type of macho charm, or concern for his safety might distract her. The sound of the siren had faded by the time she'd managed to confirm that her spare actually had air. She was trying to make sense of the diagram she found with it when Ed Simms walked up.

"Let me do that for you," he said, extending his hand for the jack.

With a sigh of mingled defeat and relief, Robin handed it over.

"I want you to come with me out to Winchesters' spread," Doc Harmon told her the next morning after he'd ended his phone call.

Since Robin had arrived at the clinic, coffee in

hand, she'd met Erline, found out where the supplies were kept and learned how to write up a bill for her time.

"Have they found more dead cattle?" she asked.

"Not as far as I know, but one of Adam's Appaloosa colts took a spill. He's like an overprotective mama with his Appies, and he wants the colt's leg checked out."

Robin glanced at Erline, who was sitting behind the desk filing her nails. She appeared to be fond of bubble gum and low-cut blouses, but she'd introduced herself with a friendly grin and she seemed competent, even though she'd admitted to a phobia toward reptiles.

"I couldn't work for a vet who treated snakes," she'd confided after she'd shown Robin how to write up an invoice for prescription pet food. "I'd quit on the spot."

"Guess that answers my question on how to get rid of you if the need arises," Doc Harmon had interjected dryly.

From the way Erline stuck out her tongue, Robin figured her co-workers enjoyed taunting each other.

"I wouldn't go anywhere with him if I were you," Erline said now as she put away her nail file. "Not since they came out with those little blue pills."

Robin's cheeks went hot with embarrassment, but the doc merely gave his receptionist a pained look. "I should sue you for sexual harassment."

Erline huffed loudly. "Save yourself the attorney fee and just give me a raise, instead."

The phone on her desk rang before he could reply. With a wink at Robin, Erline pushed the flashing button and picked up the receiver.

"Harmon Veterinary Clinic. How can I help you?"

Doc Harmon's expression turned serious. "On occasion you and I will be working closely together," he told Robin in a low voice. "I hope you don't have a problem with that."

She could feel her blush deepen. "Of course not. I came here to get experience treating livestock. I'll do my best to keep my hands off you."

For a moment his weathered face went blank with surprise, making her afraid she'd gone too far. Then he began to laugh.

"What did I miss?" Erline demanded after she'd written down an appointment in her book and ended her call. "What, what?"

"Nothing," Robin and the doc answered in unison.

"You'll do fine," he told her, still grinning. "Let's get going."

Charlie had spent the better part of the morning driving out past his brothers' ranch to check out a complaint about graffiti sprayed on the side of John Keller's barn. Ten minutes spent talking to the oldest son had solved the crime, saved Charlie a mound of paperwork and earned the boy a week's house arrest—and that was after he painted over his artwork.

The day was hot and still, the temperature high even for the end of July, and a cold soda sounded like a heck of a great idea. As he drove through the open gate to the ranch, barely glancing at the neatly painted wood sign, he chuckled at the thought of the Keller boy's expression when Charlie had confronted him with the spray can hidden in his room. The boy had gone pale, his freckles standing out like rust spots on his guilty face.

Charlie slowed the Cherokee as he drove past the two-story ranch house where Travis lived with his red-haired wife and their four children. As usual, the wide front porch was hung with baskets of brightly-colored flowers, but today the backyard swings and wading pool were empty. Rory's van was gone, too. No point in stopping.

Young Keller's misdeed reminded Charlie of some of the stunts he and his brothers had pulled as kids, but his grin faded at the memory of their father's wrath and the punishments he gave. Jason had gotten off easy today, apparently unaware of worse consequences than repainting and restriction for childish pranks. Garth Winchester hadn't believed in sparing the rod, the belt or his fists.

The sight of Adam's black pickup parked by the door to the stable was a welcome distraction, as was the idea of a cold soda from the tack room fridge. That and asking if any more dead cattle had been found were reasons enough to stop by, if Charlie had needed a reason.

When he walked into the cool, dim interior of the broodmare barn, he spotted Adam and his stepson, David, home on summer break from college. Both men were watching an Appaloosa dam and her offspring in one of the roomy stalls.

"Don't you two have any real work to do?" Charlie asked as he joined them. "I thought the Appies were supposed to be a hobby."

"Not for several years now." Adam hadn't taken his attention from the leopard-spotted colt in the stall with his mother. "Can't get rich raising cattle in this market."

Charlie knew the industry had been depressed for years. Only careful management kept many of the local ranches from going under. Even an operation as large as theirs felt the pinch.

"What's new?" he asked David as a greeting. "Still seeing that Parker girl?"

David shrugged. His lean frame had filled out some in the last year. When he'd first come to Colorado with his mother from L.A. half a decade ago, his hair was orange, his clothes were bizarre and he'd sported a chip on his shoulder the size of a cow pie. Now he looked more like a local to Charlie than some of the kids who'd been born here.

"Joey and I aren't serious," David replied, tugging on the brim of his ball cap. "We'll probably break up before I go back to school."

"You sound like your uncle," Adam remarked as

he finally turned his back on the horses. "Love-'em-and-leave-'em Winchester."

"Give the kid some time," Charlie said. "He's barely old enough to drink without getting busted, and he hasn't finished college yet. The last thing he needs to think about is getting serious about some girl looking for a ring."

Adam gave his stepson a playful thump on the shoulder. The two of them were the same height now, over six feet tall. "Your uncle's just not ready to give up the title."

"Not true." Charlie ducked into the tack room and helped himself to a soda. "If I could find a woman like your wife, I'd get hitched in a minute."

"Took me two tries to get it right, though," Adam reminded him before turning to David. "You should finish school before you decide to start a family."

If Adam had followed his own advice, he wouldn't have a daughter, Charlie thought as he downed half the soda in one swallow, but he didn't mention Kim. For the first fifteen years of her life, after her parents' divorce, she had lived here with her father. Then Kim had surprised everyone by going with her mother when she moved from Denver to Seattle.

"Don't worry about me." David looked uncomfortable. "I'm staying single."

Charlie figured it was time to show the boy a little mercy. "Have you had a chance to find out if that rat poison we found came from the shed or not?" he asked his brother.

Adam's grin faded. "Every sack's accounted for and none of the boys have noticed anything unusual. Whoever's responsible brought the poison with them. Any news on your end?"

Charlie wished he had some easy answers. "No reports of stock dying under suspicious circumstances." He rolled his shoulders to loosen the sudden tension gripping them. "I hate to say it, bro, but it's beginning to look like someone may not like you much. Have you had any problems with the help? Pissed someone off? Fired them?"

"You know this isn't the season for letting guys go." Adam traced a pattern in the wood along the top of the stall door. "We're always shorthanded until after haying and the fall roundup."

"What about that fellow from Texas you caught drinking?" David asked as he sat down on a hay bale. "He was pretty unhappy when you cut him loose."

"That was a while ago." Adam frowned. "I heard he went back home, somewhere down near Dallas."

Charlie took a notebook from his pocket. "What's his name?" he asked, pen poised. "I'll check him out, see if he's still hanging around."

Through the open stable door came the sound of a vehicle pulling up, followed a couple of moments later by the thumps of car doors shutting.

David got to his feet, and Charlie finished writing down the fired cowhand's name, Mickey Barstowe.

"Expecting anyone?" he asked as he put away the notebook and pen.

"Just Doc Harmon coming to check out Joker here. He took a spill yesterday, and his leg's a little hot."

At the mention of the vet, Charlie looked around hopefully. Sure enough, following the doc through the stable doorway was his new assistant. Both of them carried leather bags.

"Is this what our tax dollars pay for?" Doc Harmon demanded with a smile. "For you to goof off?"

"You got it," Charlie replied, glancing at Robin.

The only indication she gave that they'd already met was a small smile.

"Get that tire fixed okay?" Charlie asked her after introductions had been made all around.

Her cheeks turned pink, and she frowned. Moisture beaded her upper lip. "Yes, thank you," she said, her tone prissy.

Charlie nearly chuckled out loud. She'd be fun to tease, as long as he didn't upset her too much. She was too uptight.

"Change the tire yourself?" her boss asked when she didn't elaborate.

Her chin went up in a gesture Charlie recognized as purely defensive. "Actually, my neighbor changed it for me." It was easy to see from her glance at Charlie that the admission was hard to spit out. The woman sure came with a lot of prickles, but the sweetest fruit was surrounded by thorns.

Catching her glance, he gave her a deliberate wink before she jerked her attention away. "Always nice to have someone pitch in and help," he said in as bland a tone as he could muster.

She didn't answer. After a moment of awkward silence, Adam asked where she was from.

"Chicago," she replied, looking relieved. "I grew up there."

"You're a long way from home," David observed. He'd straightened up and puffed out his chest. Didn't the boy realize how obvious he looked, grinning at her with calf's eyes while he flexed his arms like a damn body builder?

"I wanted to get some experience with large animals," she explained. "That's my main interest."

"Well, let's look at the colt," Doc Harmon interrupted before David could ask any more questions. "Has he been limping?"

Charlie stood back and watched as both vets took their time entering the roomy stall and making sure the horses were at ease before they proceeded. Robin's nervousness seemed to vanish. Even her voice changed, going all husky and soft.

A man could get lost in the sound of it, Charlie thought, even if her appearance was strictly business. She wore a loose-fitting white blouse and long tan pants, despite the heat of the afternoon. Too bad she didn't dress like the clinic receptionist. There was a woman who knew how to draw a man's attention, even as she blinded him with color and sparkle. Everything Erline wore was short, tight and bright.

Charlie tried to imagine Robin in that type of getup and failed. It was impossible to guess her shape with the way her clothing fit. Maybe that was the point.

The other four people were busy with the horses, and he knew he'd only make her uncomfortable if he tried to talk to her now. Tipping back his head, he finished off the can of soda.

"I'll see you all later," he said to no one in particular after he'd tossed the empty can into a nearby recycling bin. "Duty calls."

Three male heads turned. Three masculine voices said goodbye. Dr. Marlowe was bent down by the colt. She never even looked up.

"Something else?" Adam asked when Charlie hesitated.

"I hope the little guy's okay," Charlie said, staring at the back of Robin's head. Her short hair was as dark as a crow's and as shiny as the paint on a new Mercedes.

Adam gave him a puzzled look. "Thanks. Keep me up to speed on the other business."

Other business? Had Adam picked up on Charlie's interest in the new vet?

His momentary blankness must have shown. "My cattle," Adam prompted him dryly. "They're dying, remember?"

"Sure thing," Charlie stuttered. "I'll let you know." He didn't dare risk another glance at Robin to see if she'd been listening to the awkward exchange. Before his oldest brother, as sharp as the rowel on a new spur and twice as scary as any bad guy, could figure out the reason Charlie had been distracted, he turned and fled.

Chapter Three

Robin pulled into her driveway and shut off the engine. She'd been on the go since six that morning, blowing out the side door with a bagel in one hand, accompanying Doc Harmon on a call first thing, assisting him in surgery back at the clinic to set a dog's shattered leg and then vaccinating a litter of kittens. In the afternoon, with a map and Erline's written instructions on the seat next to her bag, she'd made two calls on her own.

Robin frowned as her grip on the wheel tightened. She made herself glance down at the small basket of plump ripe tomatoes given to her by a grateful patient. After she'd treated the eye of an old pony with conjunctivitis, his equally ancient but much nicer owner had presented Robin with the fresh-picked tomatoes.

"Jethro usually bites Doc Harmon," the woman added, which explained why he'd sent Robin this time.

"I'm quicker on my feet than my boss," she'd replied with a wink that had earned a cackle of laughter.

Mrs. Sloan's thanks had still been echoing in her ears when she'd arrived at her next stop, feeling cocky and confident, to check on a gelding with a persistent cough.

"I asked for Doc Harmon," the rancher had snarled after she'd introduced herself and stuck out her hand. "Go back and tell him not to send a girl to do a man's job." After spitting a stream of tobacco that landed an inch from her shoe, he'd stalked away, leaving her stunned and speechless.

Robin wasn't given to tears, but her eyes had been burning when she'd let herself back out the gate. She'd figured that convincing people to trust her with their livestock might take time, given her lack of experience. Her advisor had even suggested that a shrimp like her would be better off specializing in cats or exotic birds.

What Robin hadn't expected, had not been prepared for at all, was such open rudeness, such bristling hostility, because she was a female.

She'd spent most of the drive back to town thinking of all the replies she could have made but hadn't. Even if her chance of prying open his closed mind was zero, zilch, nada, she should have tried.

Now Robin got out of her car, too tired to contemplate the possible number of chauvinists in Elbert County, and walked back down the driveway to check her mail.

Before she got to the box at the curb, Mae came out her front door. "You didn't get anything today," she called.

"I beg your pardon?" Automatically, Robin looked into the mailbox lined up with those of her neighbors. Sure enough, it was empty.

Mae came around the end of the picket fence between their two houses carrying a plate covered with plastic wrap. Today her crinkled nylon jogging suit was fluorescent pink.

"I would have left your mail on your side porch when I got ours," she said. "Did you put in a change of address? You know it takes a few days to go through."

Robin wasn't sure what to say. She didn't want to be rude, but neither did she like having her privacy invaded. Clearly she needed to establish boundaries before things got out of hand.

"Don't feel bad, dear," Mae continued. "Your friends probably don't have your new address yet, but you'll be hearing from them before you know it."

Robin couldn't think of anyone who'd contact her, unless it was about some bill she'd overlooked when she left Chicago. She'd kept to herself and with good reason. Did pariahs have friends?

Mae was studying Robin through her thick lenses. "Long day, huh? Ed was up early, and he saw you leave this morning. You look washed-out. A little blusher would give your cheeks some color.''

''Is that so?'' Robin managed, feeling slightly overwhelmed. She didn't bother to explain that she never wore makeup anymore. Mae might ask why not. Her own bright cheeks were a testament to the power of cosmetics.

''You know a bagel isn't enough breakfast, if that's the only thing you had,'' Mae went on in a scolding tone. She held out the plate she'd been carrying. ''Here's some chicken salad for your dinner. I made extra. You shouldn't eat a heavy meal too close to your bedtime.''

Robin looked down at the nicely arranged slices of chicken breast and tomato on a bed of crisp lettuce. A little cup of dressing was tucked next to a hard-boiled egg cut in wedges and sprinkled lightly with paprika.

Her mouth began to water. Lunch had been half a peanut butter sandwich eaten on the run. How could she accept the salad and then tell her obviously well-intentioned neighbor to butt out?

''Thank you.'' Robin caved in without a struggle. ''It looks wonderful.'' She could always set boundaries later.

''Don't worry about returning the plate,'' Mae said as she walked away. ''There's no hurry. And don't stay up too late. You need your rest so you don't get sick.''

Robin was never sick, but she made a mental note

to close the front curtains later, so the light from her television didn't shine through the window.

By the time she'd finished the salad, a glass of the sun tea she'd made the day before and a piece of leftover garlic bread she'd found in the refrigerator, she felt as if she just might survive. She tidied the kitchen and flopped down on the couch with a sigh. Grabbing the remote, she switched on a TV game show, but she couldn't concentrate. Instead she went back over her boss's reaction to the message Robin had relayed from Elmer Babcock.

Doc Harmon had merely shaken his head dismissively. "Don't worry about it," he'd said. "The man's head is like a four-fingered bowling ball, solid as a rock and with too many holes."

Erline had snorted loudly at his quip, but Robin barely managed a smile.

"It was probably my fault for not warning you," he'd added with a paternal pat on her shoulder. "We'll bide our time. Sooner or later the old coot will need you more than you need him."

At least he hadn't suggested she not go back.

Now Robin switched channels restlessly and then turned off the TV. Running into the reality of that kind of gender bias hurt more than she would have figured. Especially after the warm welcome she'd received from people like Adam Winchester.

Both he and David, the younger man she thought must be Adam's son, had seemed genuinely pleased to meet her. They were both rugged, attractive males, something she could appreciate in a totally platonic way. David had even offered to show her around the area when she had time, but she'd been so busy examining her patient, a darling colt with spots like a dalmatian, that she didn't think she'd even replied. Not that it mattered. She was too old for David to be interested in her. He was just being polite.

She tried to block her mind from thinking about the other brother, the sheriff she'd met before. He was there at the stable when she and Doc arrived, but he'd barely spoken to Robin and he'd left right away.

Not that she'd noticed, of course. Nor had she been disappointed that he hadn't said goodbye to her, either.

By Friday Robin was actually looking forward to the weekend, even though she loved her job. She'd be on call, which was both exciting and scary.

"You've earned a break. Besides, I have paperwork to finish on Saturday, so I'll be here at the clinic most of the day, anyway," Doc Harmon told her as she was getting ready to leave work. "Go out tonight. Relax, have fun."

"I've got some unpacking left to do." She pictured the lone box of books sitting in the bedroom.

"Oh, too exciting," Erline drawled, waving her freshly painted nails to dry them. "How can you stand it?"

Robin ignored her jibe, but Doc Harmon swiveled

his head. "And what are you doing this weekend?" he asked the receptionist. "Got a hot date?"

"In this town?" she shot back. "Are you kidding? The men around here are either married or they're your age. Or both." She rolled her eyes and fanned herself. "Be still my heart."

He peered at her over the tops of his glasses while Robin waited expectantly. "Or they're just too darned picky," he drawled.

Erline blew a bubble and then she turned her attention to Robin. "My girlfriend Carol and I are going out for dinner and a couple of drinks. Want to come along?"

Robin was about to refuse when Doc spoke up for her. "Good idea. She'll go."

Why did everyone she'd met think they had to help run her life? "I have things to do," she protested.

He raised his eyebrows, his expression stern. "You need to get out, meet people. Bring us more business. Charlie's Heart is a good place to start."

"Charlie's what?" she echoed.

"It's a restaurant and lounge," Erline interjected. "Food's good, and they've got live music on the weekends, even though the dance floor's the size of my desk."

Oh, great, Robin thought. A bar with music and dancing. Men on the prowl. "I don't think so."

Erline ducked her head and pulled open a file drawer. "Your loss."

"I've got to call the lab." Doc Harmon headed for the back room with a folder under his arm.

Despite Erline's colorful appearance and wise-cracking attitude, Robin liked her. Beneath her cocky veneer, the older woman seemed to have a genuine affection for the animals they treated. She shrugged off Robin's mistakes and swept aside her apologies with a smile or a joke.

Robin hated the idea that she might have hurt the older woman's feelings. And Doc was right: Robin owed it to him and the practice to get out and meet people.

"If the invitation is still open, I'd like to go," she said hesitantly.

Erline's head popped back up, and she blew a bubble. "Great. We'll pick you up at eight, so we don't miss happy hour. Carol's a hoot. You'll like her." She studied Robin with a considering expression as she worked her gum. "Wear something more, you know, feminine."

Fashion advice from a Barbie doll look-alike, even one with a heart of gold, wasn't exactly what Robin wanted to hear. Clothes weren't a priority of hers. "How dressy is this place?"

Erline pursed her lips. "Oh, people wear just about anything, Western, casual, whatever." Her expression brightened. "I'll bet we're about the same size except for our height. Want to borrow something of mine?"

Today she was wearing an electric-blue leather miniskirt paired with a striped peasant blouse in some shiny fabric that dipped low in the front and clung to her generous curves like a coat of paint. Matching feather and rhinestone earrings swung wildly whenever she moved her head. If she and Robin were the same size, so were Texas and Rhode Island.

''No, thanks. That's really nice of you to offer, but I'll find something.'' Robin hoped her smile offset her hasty refusal.

For a moment she thought Erline was going to argue. From the other room she heard a fit of coughing, and she wondered if Doc had heard them.

The phone on Erline's desk rang. ''See you later,'' she told Robin with a wink as she reached for the receiver.

Robin left the clinic with mixed feelings about the evening ahead. By seven-thirty she was kicking herself for agreeing to go. On the bed before her was every garment she owned that was remotely suitable. Not only wouldn't anything there measure up to Erline's assessment of feminine attire, even Robin was painfully aware of the lack.

Hands on hips, she stared down at the skimpy selection. She'd ruled out the cotton slacks and tailored cotton blouses she'd bought for work, the worn jeans and faded T-shirts, the shorts she saved for hot weather. That left two dresses she wore to church and one with a halter top she'd bought on impulse for a party back in school. She'd changed her mind about attending and the tag was still attached. No Returns, it said. All Sales Final.

What had she been thinking when she bought it? The dress was shorter than she liked and the back dipped too low for her to wear a bra with it. At least the color was plain dark blue, not showy at all, and she had sandals that would match it.

Decision made, she was dressed and ready fifteen minutes early. Restlessly she paced the small living room, watching through the window for Erline's car so she could go outside as soon as the other two women pulled into the driveway and save them the trouble of getting out. She would have waited on the porch except that Mae and Ed were working in their yard and she didn't feel like chatting with them—or answering Mae's inevitable questions.

Robin hadn't yet returned their plate. Aunt Dot had taught her never to return a dish empty, so maybe tomorrow she'd make some brownies if it wasn't too hot to run the oven.

Before she could speculate further, a shiny red Honda turned into her driveway with two women inside. Recognizing Erline in the passenger seat, Robin grabbed her purse. Out of habit, she locked the side door after her and waved at her neighbors as Erline got out of the car to let Robin climb in the back. Erline was wearing a tight sleeveless red knit dress with matching hoop earrings. She glanced at Robin's outfit, but didn't comment.

"You don't get carsick, do you?" Erline asked as she pulled the seat forward. "Because if you do, I can ride back there, but we're only two minutes from Charlie's.''

"I'll be fine." As she climbed in, Robin nodded shyly at the woman behind the wheel. "Hi."

"Carol, this is Robin," Erline said. "And vice versa."

"Nice to meet you," Carol drawled. She had long brown hair with lighter streaks and a round, pretty face that was carefully made up.

"Carol's from Atlanta, in case you can't tell." Erline's brassy blond hair sprang away from her face in waves and was puffed up on top. Riding in the car with the two other women, Robin felt like a plain little sparrow trapped in a parakeet cage.

Not an especially flattering image for any of them.

"How long have you lived here?" Robin asked Carol as they turned the corner at the end of her street.

"Ten years." Carol glanced into the rearview mirror. "I teach secondary school in Elizabeth. Erline tells me you're from Chicago."

"Born and bred."

"I went to Chicago once on vacation with my family, but I didn't care for it much," Carol replied, turning another corner. She pronounced her *I* as *Ah*. Robin was surprised her accent was still so strong after a decade spent in Colorado.

Before Robin had the chance to think up a suitable response, Carol whipped the car over to an empty spot by the curb. Other vehicles already lined both sides of the street.

Robin hadn't driven down this way or had time to do much exploring yet, but now she saw the sign in front of the big one-story building that appeared to be their destination. Despite the waning daylight, Charlie's Heart pulsated in red and pink neon. When Erline opened the car door, Robin could hear the rhythmic throb of music coming from inside the club.

The sign made her think of the sheriff. Charlie must be a common nickname in Waterloo. Would he be here tonight or was he at home with a family of his own? She hadn't noticed a ring on his finger, but of course that didn't mean anything and she hadn't really been looking.

An image of little cowkids wearing miniature badges and cowboy hats made her smother a grin. Then a gorgeous blonde slid into Robin's mental picture and tucked her arm through Sheriff Winchester's.

Robin blinked away the image as Erline got out of the Honda and smoothed down her skirt. Carol wore black pants and a long top that flattered her plump figure. Gold bangle bracelets sparkled in the light and her perfume reeked of name brand exclusivity. It made Robin want to sneeze.

"Hey, ladies!" called out a cowboy-type as he pulled open the front door to Charlie's. He was wearing pressed jeans and a bright turquoise shirt with pearl snaps and a lightning bolt across the chest. Two other men, similarly dressed, were with him. All three wore black Stetsons and western boots.

"Hi, Bobby Joe." Erline waved at the men before

they disappeared inside. She turned back to Carol and Robin. "Looks like a good crowd tonight."

"It's always like this when they have a decent band and Charlie sings," Carol replied, raising her voice over the sound of the music.

Butterflies danced in Robin's midsection, and she slowed her pace as an attack of nerves hit her. What had she been thinking? She would much rather be at home in her bathrobe with a rented movie and bowl of popcorn.

As if she could sense Robin's sudden reluctance, Erline hooked an arm through hers and tugged her forward. She spoke directly into Robin's ear. "Don't worry, we'll look out for you, and everyone's real friendly here."

"Thanks," Robin muttered, her mouth dry, as Erline turned her loose. Taking a deep breath, she followed her companions through the front door. It was painted red and adorned with an elaborate brass knob in the shape of entwined hearts. To Robin they might as well have been gargoyles.

Even inside the club, the music from a very good sound system wasn't overwhelming. Trying to adjust her vision to the dimness of the interior, Robin bumped into Carol, who'd stopped at the hostess podium. Carol flashed her a smile as Erline spoke to an attractive young woman in a red jumpsuit.

In moments the three of them were seated at a round table on one side of a large room. The chair backs were heart-shaped red leather. In the middle of the table a ruby glass candle holder gave a romantic glow. The overall decor of the room had a Western theme, which wasn't surprising, but it also managed to appear both intimate and trendy.

A small stage was at one end of the room, on it an elaborate set of drums, several speakers and some other sound equipment. A panel of lights hung overhead. The dance floor was slightly larger than Erline had described, and a bar carved of dark wood ran along the opposite wall. Behind the bar was a mirrored wall with glass shelves filled with liquor bottles. Along the top ran a neon border in red, pink and gold. Many of the bar stools were already occupied, as were most of the tables.

Several racks of antlers adorned one paneled wall, but at least there weren't any mounted animal heads. Through an arched doorway, Robin could see pool tables in another room and more people.

"I'm having the prime rib," Erline announced, sliding aside her unopened menu. "How about you two?"

They all ordered the house specialty. By the time they'd finished eating, the place was nearly full and the band members were onstage, setting up the rest of their equipment. A man adjusted the mikes while two guitar players tuned their instruments. A redheaded woman in tight green jeans and a matching satin shirt that dripped with fringe was talking to several couples seated near the stage as she fluffed out her mane of hair.

Robin tried to keep straight the names of everyone she'd met as they stopped by the table, but she finally gave up. Between her two companions, they knew practically everyone in town and the surrounding area. Robin felt as though in the last hour she'd been introduced to the entire adult population of Elbert County.

Their waitress had just cleared their dishes, brought fresh beers and a refill on Robin's iced tea when the bank of colored lights above the stage went on. The drummer gave an introductory drum roll and a trim, muscular man in dark jeans and a striped shirt under a leather vest bounded up the stage steps. When he turned to face the room, the audience burst into applause and cheers. Unlike the rest of the band, the MC's head was bare.

Robin's breath lodged in her chest and her heart seemed to miss a beat as the stage lighting illuminated the man's handsome face. When Erline stuck her fingers in her mouth and whistled, loud and shrill, Robin nearly bolted from her chair.

The noise finally died down when he held up his hands, grinning broadly, and began to speak.

"Welcome, welcome. This is my place and you're all my guests, so everyone have yourself a great time. While you're here, I'm just your host, Charlie Winchester, so for tonight at least, try to forget my other job, okay? Thanks for coming."

While Robin stared, unable to shift her gaze away from his image, bathed in a golden glow, he turned and signaled the band, which immediately began to play a fast-paced and familiar country song. The redhead marked the beat on a tambourine, the fringe on her shirt jumping in time with the music, as couples poured onto the dance floor. Charlie came back down the steps, stopping every few feet to greet people and shake their hands as he worked his way slowly around the perimeter of the room.

"What do you think?" Erline demanded, pitching her voice so she could be heard above the music.

Robin had been watching his progress, unable to tear her gaze away. Her cheeks flamed at Erline's question. Good grief, had she been that obvious, gaping at the sheriff as though she'd never seen a man before?

"I-I beg your p-pardon?" she stammered, trying to bluff. "Think about what?"

"This place!" Erline shouted, her gesture encompassing their surroundings. "Not bad for a little hick town, huh?"

"Hey!" someone said from behind Robin. "What are you saying, E? We're in the center of the known world here, didn't you know that?"

To Robin's utter relief, Erline swiveled around in her chair and began talking to the speaker while another man leaned across the table and asked Carol to dance. When she nodded and got to her feet, Robin ducked her head.

She took a long swallow of her iced tea. Too bad she couldn't hold some of the cubes to her burning cheeks. At least Erline was still busy and had no doubt forgotten all about her question to Robin.

"Excuse me." A deep, familiar voice spoke from somewhere above Robin's lowered head as an outstretched hand appeared in her line of vision. "May I have this dance?"

Charlie had seen her come into the club with the other two women, and he'd managed to give Erline a thumbs-up behind Robin's back before he'd ducked into the kitchen. He'd owe Erline a favor, but he wasn't worried that she'd take advantage. One fixed ticket wasn't going to corrupt either of them.

Perhaps it had been pretty egotistical for him to think he had to hide in order not to spook the new vet into leaving, but a man couldn't be too careful when he had an attractive woman in his sights. He hadn't felt this rush of interest in a long while, and he didn't intend for her to slip away before they'd shared at least one dance.

He knew how to take no from a woman, even though he'd never had to, not that he could remember. And of course he would never force his company on one who was genuinely uninterested. If she truly didn't share the pull he felt, he'd survive, but he wanted the chance to find out.

While he looked down at her upturned face and waited for her answer, he could see the flare in her eyes of more than just surprise. What was she nervous about?

Not him. He was as harmless as a descented skunk.

He nearly spoke the words aloud. Then her lips firmed and her chin came up, more like she'd decided to swallow a dose of quinine rather than take a turn around the floor with a guy who wasn't likely to mash her toes too badly.

"Okay," she said, solemn-faced, as she slid back her chair.

The dress she was wearing was dark and plain, the neckline revealing only a hint of cleavage. Somehow the outfit's clean lines suited her, just like her short hair and bare face. He'd bet her underwear was plain cotton, too. Someday he'd see for himself, if he had a vote.

Charlie kept the smile plastered on his face while she got to her feet. The top of her head might brush his chin if his knees were bent. He'd bet her hair, as dark and shiny as obsidian, smelled as clean as the wind. In a moment he'd know.

Her gaze met his, and she took a deep breath. He gave himself points for not letting his attention waver from her dark eyes.

"Shall we?" he asked, indicating the dance floor.

It was a rhetorical question, but she hesitated. Before she could change her mind, Charlie cupped her elbow and urged her toward the other couples. She hadn't said no, not yet, and for tonight at least he had no intention of giving her the chance.

Chapter Four

As Robin allowed Sheriff Winchester to escort her onto the crowded dance floor, the upbeat tempo of the music shifted and slowed. The stage lighting dimmed, leaving a single spot shining down on the redhead. With the guitars weeping softly, she lifted her face to the light and began to sing a ballad in a pure, sweet voice.

The sheriff released Robin's elbow and held out his arms. "Come on, honey," he urged. "It's just a dance."

Her touch on his shoulder was tentative, but he captured her other hand in a firm grip, entwining their fingers. His palm was warm. As she stared at their joined hands, he slid his other arm around her waist and guided her gently into the music.

She had no choice but to follow his lead. Her body was stiff, her chest tight.

"Sheriff," she began, her chin up.

"Charlie," he corrected her gently. "I'm wearing my other hat tonight."

Her gaze lifted automatically to his bare head. "No you're not."

Oh, God, what a dumb thing to say. Her cheeks went hot as he grinned down at her, and she hoped the lighting was too dim for him to see her blush.

"Good point." As relaxed as she was nervous, he swung her easily around. She looked past him to her empty table. Erline must be dancing, too.

To Robin's surprise, she didn't stumble once as she matched her steps to Charlie's. He was easy to follow, his movements as smooth as maple syrup oozing from a pitcher. Her confidence rose and she began to loosen up.

He must have felt the change, because he looked into her eyes and then he leaned down, tucking her closer. His cheek touched her hair and their bodies brushed when he turned her again. His presence surrounded her. They moved across the floor as easily as though they'd been practicing for years.

Robin couldn't remember the last time she'd been held by a man.

Held down.

The image came back, stark and painful. She stumbled, her foot crunching hard on Charlie's boot. He managed to catch her before she could fall and humiliate herself in front of him and the other couples around them.

"Are you okay?" he asked, steadying her.

"I...I'm sorry." She swallowed. "I'm fine, really." Their feet had stopped moving, but their bodies still swayed in time to the music. Her gaze was fixed on his chest pocket, where the fabric had been sewn so the stripes formed a chevron. "Uh, did I hurt you?" Tears threatened, but she blinked them back, the way she always did—teeth clenched to keep the emotion inside.

Charlie bent his head. "Naw, I'm okay, too," he said softly. His breath against her ear sent a shiver right through her, distracting her. She tried to ignore it. "I always wear steel-toed boots when I dance, just in case," he added. "Women are always trying to cripple me for one reason or another."

Robin managed a shaky smile.

From the stage, the singer hit a high, pure note, held it and then soared again.

"She has a lovely voice," Robin said, glad for the excuse to change the subject.

Charlie cocked his head as the guitarists played a musical bridge. "Yeah, she does. I'll tell her you said so."

"Is she your girlfriend?" Robin blurted.

"Oh, Rory will get such a kick out of that," he replied with a grin. "She's married to my next older brother, Travis." His arms tightened and he shifted Robin around to avoid a collision with another couple. "I don't think you've met him yet." Charlie's tone held a question.

Robin shook her head. "I've only met Adam and his son."

"His son?" Charlie echoed.

"David."

"David Major, stepson," he corrected. "You'd need a program to keep us all straight." He glanced at the stage. "Rory's got four kids. The oldest is nine. She was feeling a little housebound and the band needed a singer. Everyone's happy."

"She's beautiful," Robin said sincerely as she watched the other woman lift up her mike and begin to sing again. "How I envy people with families."

"You don't have one?"

She hadn't realized she'd spoken her thought aloud. "Uh, no. Just my aunt, but she died while I was in college." Talking about herself made Robin uncomfortable.

"I'm sorry. So you put yourself through veterinary school. That must have been difficult."

She shrugged, seeing no reason to explain that her aunt had left her the money for her tuition. "The training is hard anyway, but maybe I had it easier than the ones with families."

"What do you mean?" he asked. He seemed genuinely interested.

"Well, I had fewer distractions." She had to think for a moment. "Not having to deal with anyone else's needs or going home for weekend visits or remembering to call or to write. I could focus on my studies.''

"Maybe so," he replied, "but it sounds awfully lonely to me."

"You don't miss what you haven't had." As soon as the words were out, she regretted them. They revealed too much.

Charlie didn't reply, just pulled her close again with their joined hands nestled between them. Without conversation to distract her, Robin was more aware of the warmth of his body, the faint scent of his cologne, even the steady beat of his heart.

She was sure her own pulse must be galloping like a runaway mustang. Was it nerves or attraction or a mix of both? She should ignore the temptation to lean into his warmth for just a moment longer. She needed to pull away, keep a safe distance between them.

While she was losing the battle with her own weakness, he lifted his head and came to a stop. Only then did she realize that the music had faded to a whisper. Their dance was over.

Applause burst out around them and Charlie released Robin's hand so they could join in. Up on the stage, Rory was taking her bows. She tossed back her flaming hair, making the fringe on her sleeve shimmy against the emerald satin of her shirt. She was tall and slim, making it hard to believe she was the mother of four.

Once again, as Robin stood next to Charlie, she felt like a plain little bird hovering at the edge of a world vibrating with color and energy. For a moment, as the band began another number, she nearly forgot that going unnoticed was her preference.

Charlie cupped his hand under her elbow, his fingers warm and rough against her skin, and escorted her back to the table where both of her companions were already seated. They both greeted Charlie with welcoming smiles.

"Ladies." He pulled out Robin's chair. "Thanks for the dance."

Her knees shook as she sat down.

"Maybe you'll save me another one," he suggested. "I've got chores to do, but I'll be back later on." Without waiting for a reply, he left them, cutting through the couples still milling around on the dance floor.

"So!" Erline exclaimed as she and Carol both leaned forward expectantly. "I didn't realize you and our local hunk were so tight."

"I've only met him through work," Robin replied, trying not to sound defensive. "I don't know him all that well."

"I'll bet Charlie makes a point of checking out every new arrival, as long as she's female," Carol said with a knowing look at Erline. "Our sheriff is a ladies' man, all right, a real love-'em-and-leave-'em kind of guy."

Erline sipped her beer with a thoughtful expression. "I wouldn't say that, exactly." She looked at Robin. "Oh, don't get the wrong idea. He's like any single guy. He plays the field and he likes to flirt, but he wouldn't hurt a fly, not intentionally.''

"It really doesn't matter to me." Robin shouldn't have cared one way or the other, but her mood deflated like a leaky raft.

So it wasn't that he found her attractive. She was just new in town. He must keep busy during tourist season.

The drummer pounded out the beat of a lively Brooks and Dunn number, distracting her. A cheer went up, followed by a rush toward the already crowded floor.

In the confusion that followed, all three women were asked to dance. The older, slightly paunchy man who approached Robin looked familiar, as did his oversize gray hat—more fifteen gallon than ten. She couldn't remember his name but, afraid to risk offending someone she might have already met this evening, she accepted his offer and allowed him to pull her into the sea of writhing bodies.

By the time the rousing number was over, she was breathless from the exertion. Her partner had been surprisingly light on his feet, and he'd taught her a few steps before returning her to the table with a parting grin.

For the next half dozen numbers, all fast dances, she didn't sit down at all. Nor did she see Charlie, except for one quick glimpse of him lugging a crate behind the bar.

"Man, I'm parched!" Erline cried dramatically,

collapsing into her chair when the band finally announced a break. Her hair was sticking out on one side, and her face was shiny. "Where's the waitress?" she demanded. "We need another round."

Erline glanced at Robin's iced tea glass, empty except for a lone lemon wedge in the bottom. "How about you?" she asked, taking her lip gloss and a small mirror from her bag. "Want to share a pitcher, since Carol's driving?"

Robin shook her head. She rarely drank. One never knew when an emergency might come up. "Sorry, but I'd better stick with this." She lifted her glass, wishing there was some ice left in the bottom. At least her sleeveless dress was fairly comfortable.

Despite the slowly turning paddle fans overhead, the temperature in the room was climbing. The place was packed with bodies. Every chair and bar stool was taken and people stood around in small groups as more kept arriving.

Carol was fanning herself with a paper coaster, her round cheeks rosy with color. Erline kept lifting her hair away from her neck, disrupting the style. For several moments, the three of them tried without success to flag down a waiter. With the band on a break and the dance floor nearly empty, the staff was swamped with orders.

"I'd go to the bar myself, but it's ten deep over there," Erline grumbled. Suddenly her grimace lifted and she sat up straighter. "Way to go!" she exclaimed.

Their dark-haired waitress appeared with a tray holding a sweating pitcher of amber liquid, two fresh glasses of iced tea, garnished with lemon wedges and mint sprigs and a basket of popcorn. As she served everything, all three women reached for their money.

"Put that away," the waitress said, pitching her voice above the sounds of the band that had returned from their break. "It's on the house."

If this was the way Charlie treated his customers, no wonder the place was packed, Robin thought.

"Do they do this often?" she asked as Erline poured a beer and Carol dug into the bowl of popcorn.

"No way." Erline took a long drink. "It's because of you. Apparently you've got an in with management."

"Let's keep her," Carol replied, mouth full. "Think of the money we could save."

Robin glanced from one to the other, not entirely sure they weren't just ribbing her. "What do you mean?"

A warm hand closed over her shoulder. "Having a good time?" asked a deep, familiar voice.

She turned her head to look up at Charlie, but he'd bent down to talk to her, so they ended up nearly nose to nose. His gaze shifted to her mouth and he leaned closer still, as though he were going to kiss her. His fingers tightened on her shoulder.

Robin froze, forgetting to protest or even to breathe. Her lips tingled in helpless anticipation.

"Not here." His voice was gruff, for her ears alone. "Not the first time."

As he straightened abruptly, Robin could only gawk, wondering if she'd heard right. For someone who enjoyed flirting, his expression seemed awfully serious.

Vaguely she heard her companions thanking him for the free refreshments. At least they hadn't heard his comment or they'd tease her even more.

"So you're all having a good time tonight?" he asked, removing his hand from Robin's shoulder.

Carol saluted him with her schooner and batted her eyes dramatically. "Will the band be playing a ladies' choice anytime soon?"

"I'll see to it," he replied, his grin back in place.

Someone shouted his name from a nearby table. "Gotta go," he said, and then his gaze met Robin's. "Don't forget what I said."

As soon as Charlie's back was turned, Erline leaned across the table. "What did he mean?" she demanded. "What did he say to you when he was snuggled so close?"

Robin managed an exaggerated shrug. "Beats me." It was the truth. If Charlie's comment was an example of flirting, Colorado-style, she had a lot of catching up to do.

By the time the band had played a couple more numbers, Robin was starting to get tired. It had been a stressful week, the beginning of a new page in her life, and the adrenaline surge she'd felt from that first dance with Charlie had long since faded. She was about to ask Erline if they could leave when the stage lights went down, followed by a burst of scattered applause.

A shadowy male figure ascended the darkened steps, carrying a guitar. A single spotlight came up as he slung the strap over his shoulder and faced the audience. Robin recognized him immediately despite a cordless mike partially hiding his familiar smile. Apparently, the sheriff-dash-club-owner-dash-ladies'-man had yet another hat in his collection.

Most of the couples who'd been dancing drifted off the floor and the rest stood facing the stage. Except for a few lowered voices and the muffled snick of billiard balls colliding in the next room, the room went quiet.

Robin glanced at Erline, but for once the blonde was silent. Her attention was on Charlie as he began to play.

"First I get cold," he sang, "then hot." His voice tripped easily over the notes as he strummed the guitar.

Robin took the opportunity to study him without worrying about being caught gawking like a groupie. He was one of the most attractive men she'd ever seen.

Clearly he was having a great time on the stage. Well, why not? He must know everyone in Elbert County, and he had a pretty decent voice.

"What a hunk." Carol sighed, sipping her iced tea.

Charlie crossed the stage, his tone playful now, his hand pressed against his side as he described a pain that must be love. He came down the steps and began working the room while the band played backup. People turned in their seats to watch his progress, and it seemed to Robin that he kept glancing straight at her.

Yeah, right. She'd bet most of the women were thinking the same thing. It was just part of the act.

As though he were performing in his own living room he lifted the guitar high and wiggled his hips. A woman in a low-cut sequined top reached out and grabbed his arm. Without missing a note, he bent over her hand and gave it a smacking kiss. She said something as he straightened, and he inserted a laugh right into the lyrics.

He stopped to nod at a few other people, and Robin heaved a sigh of relief. How silly to think she had made some kind of lasting impression on him, just because he'd asked her to dance.

His looks, his charm, that flirtatious manner that appeared so natural—it was all good for business. He met women all the time. He would hardly remember Robin.

She took a long pull on her iced tea. As she set down her glass, she looked up. Charlie had abandoned the circular path he'd been taking and was headed straight toward her table as he repeated the song's refrain, "It must be love."

She stiffened, eyes widening. He *was* staring straight at her!

Interaction with his audience might well be part of the show, but the idea that he might single her out, expecting her to play along and even manage some witty response, made her want to slip out of her seat and hide in the ladies' room.

Being the center of attention always terrified her. Her mind went blank, she blushed and stammered, her tongue got thick. She made embarrassing mistakes. Reciting in class had been agony. She'd never had dreams of performing, certainly not in front of anyone. Unless she was forced to deliver a lecture on disease prevention or animal health care, she avoided the spotlight.

Scarcely breathing, she willed him to change direction, to head for one of the gorgeous women she'd seen flirting with him earlier. Someone actually *trying* to get Charlie's attention.

"Uh-oh," Erline whispered loudly as Carol scooted her chair around in order to watch his progress better. "How'd he find out about that parking ticket I didn't pay?"

Carol snickered and elbowed her. He was only a few feet away now, his smile lazy as he neared the end of the song. A girl with a tumble of blond hair stood up, but he ignored her.

Was this what he'd meant when he'd told Robin earlier that he'd be back?

Panic swept over her. She should have slunk away when she'd had the chance. Escaping now was impossible.

He stopped right in front of her table and his hand stilled on the guitar.

"What else could it be?" he asked, eyes brimming with mischief, dimples flashing. While Robin willed the floor to open up and swallow her, everyone shouted out, "It must be love!"

Charlie leaned over Robin. "It must be love." His voice had dropped to a whisper, but his mike picked up every word.

In the moment of silence that followed, she stared into his brown eyes, unable to look away. Then some-one started cheering and the room erupted, shattering the spell. Charlie spun around and thrust his arms into the air, acknowledging the applause. He was quite a showman, that was for darned sure.

"Way to go!" Erline cried out, clapping madly.

Relieved that the moment had passed and no one seemed to be staring at her, Robin sucked in a shaky breath. She pressed a hand to her fluttery stomach and waited for the band to start their number so the danc-ing would resume and Charlie would go away.

Instead he turned back toward her and addressed her by name.

Now what?

"Would you mind standing up for a moment?" he asked, his amplified voice blasting the question to the four corners of the room. "I'd like to introduce you to my friends."

Swallowing, Robin sent him a pleading look that he ignored. Instead he gave her a smile of encouragement. What did hams like Charlie know about stage fright?

Cheeks burning, knees wobbling, she took his hand and got to her feet with only a minimum of awkwardness. He stood calmly beside her, grinning at an endless sea of faces, while she contemplated crawling beneath the table. As a tremor of nervousness went through her, he raised their linked hands into the air like a referee with a winning prizefighter.

"Allow me to introduce one of Waterloo's newest residents," he said. "Dr. Robin Marlowe has joined Doc Harmon's veterinary practice. So now that you've all met Robin, don't be strangers. Drop by the clinic to say hi. Give her a call when you need a vet."

Robin's smile felt wooden as the silence stretched awkwardly. She was dying to escape, but his grip on her hand wouldn't let her go. After a round of tepid clapping, he finally allowed her to sit back down.

"That wasn't so bad, was it?" he asked. "Next time you and I can sing a duet."

"There's an idea," Erline interjected.

"Thank you," Robin muttered through lips that were stiff with shyness. "But I don't think so."

His gesture had been a thoughtful one. He couldn't know how self-conscious she was in front of crowds, especially when he didn't have a bashful bone in his extremely attractive male body.

"You're very welcome." Still smiling, he gave her a small bow while Carol thumped her hand repeatedly over her heart, rolling her eyes, and Erline fanned herself.

One of the bartenders came up and said something in Charlie's ear. He glanced toward the bar with a frown, said something in reply, and then the two of them walked away, still talking as the band began to play a lively instrumental.

"Does he always do that when someone new comes here for the first time?" Robin asked her table companions.

"Not that I can remember," Erline replied. "He might introduce someone if they're celebrating a real milestone, like a twenty-fifth anniversary, but he sure doesn't serenade them first! And usually it's the waiters who sing for birthdays and stuff, but not when there's live music."

Robin shrugged. "Maybe it will bring the clinic some new business."

"Like we need that," Erline snorted. "We're busy now. Especially with someone out there poisoning cattle."

Carol's eyes grew round. "What? When did it happen?" she demanded. "I didn't see anything in the newspaper."

As Erline leaned closer to fill her in over the sound of the music, Robin smothered a yawn behind her hand. She felt as though she'd been in surgery for hours. She'd had no idea when Erline invited her out for dinner and a drink that they were planning to make a night of it.

Erline glanced at her as she fought another yawn. "You want to go?"

It was getting late. "If you don't mind," Robin replied apologetically. "I'm afraid I'm not used to staying up unless I'm delivering a new foal."

"I'm ready, too, if you are," Carol said. "I'm going antiquing with my cousin in the morning, and she likes to get an early start."

Tipping back her head, Erline drained the last of her beer. "So many men I didn't dance with tonight," she remarked with mock regret, raising her empty schooner. "Guess the rest of you boys will have to wait."

Seated behind his desk the next morning with a steaming mug of sludge at his elbow, Charlie leafed through the stack of written reports from the week. The Waterloo crime wave included a missing cat, two teenagers caught shoplifting a CD, a complaint about a neighbor playing loud music, a stolen truck, a couple of burglaries and his brothers' dead cattle.

Charlie opened the file and glanced over the pitiful bit of information he'd collected so far. He'd interviewed the ranch hands and the neighbors, but no one had seen anything suspicious. The clerks at the co-op couldn't recall any strangers buying rat poison. Except for a smudged impression of a tire track Charlie had taken at the scene and a lab report confirming the cause of death, he had nothing to go on. No one else in the county had filed a report on dead cattle. Unless the incident was repeated, and he hoped to God it wasn't, he'd pretty much come up against a blank wall.

Frustrated, Charlie closed the file with a slap. Why'd he let himself be talked into running for this job when Sheriff Hathaway retired?

Because he'd hated the idea of a bully like Owen Bassett running unopposed, that was why. And Charlie had never thought he would actually win, not when the sum total of his experience in law enforcement had been playing cops and robbers as a kid. When he'd first taken over, plenty of people said he'd run on the popularity ticket—or his brother Adam's coattails.

Charlie was learning, though. He liked to think he was slowly changing folks' minds about the job he was doing. He'd taken several seminars in Denver, he put in a lot of hours despite running the club, too, and he worked hard to be a good sheriff.

He turned his chair to face the window and the back parking lot. He'd much rather be thinking about the skittish new vet than trying to figure out who'd killed helpless animals and why.

Hell, maybe he should go hunt for Mrs. Meriweather's lost cat. That was a case he might have a decent chance of solving. Feeling the pangs of a headache coming on, he pinched the bridge of his nose between two fingers.

The phone rang out front, but the weekend dispatcher didn't transfer the call to him. Except for the faint sound of her radio playing classic rock and a car with a cranky muffler driving past, the office was quiet. The two-cell jail in the back of the building was, as usual, empty.

He hoped it stayed that way. Quiet. Slow. Normally he slept as if he'd been hit in the head, and more than once his brothers had taken advantage of that to play pranks on him. One time they'd shaved his head while he slept, which had earned all three of them a whipping.

Charlie smothered a yawn and contemplated the black goo in his mug. Hell, he could see his exhausted reflection.

He'd left the club before closing last night, early for him on a weekend, but then he'd lain awake for hours. This morning he'd been too grumpy to stop in at Emma's Café for his usual Saturday breakfast of biscuits and country gravy. He'd settled instead for the mysterious brew left here in the pot by the night deputy.

Charlie tipped back his mug and nearly gagged on the taste, his stomach doing a dip and roll that left him swallowing hard. Cops might be used to drinking battery acid, but that was just one more part of the job to which Charlie hadn't yet fully adjusted.

Hearing voices in the outer office, he set the mug back down and flipped open a file so he'd look busy. Then he glanced up expectantly and waited.

Hell, he needn't have bothered.

"Hey, bro," he said, standing up. "You, too," he

greeted Travis, who'd come in behind Adam. "You two slumming?"

Neither cracked a smile in response to Charlie's quip. They stopped inside the doorway, hands jammed in their pockets, hat brims pulled low. Neither spoke.

Neither had to.

"Damn," Charlie exclaimed, reaching around behind them to shut the door. "More dead cattle?"

"You got it," Adam replied.

Charlie cleared a stack of files off one chair and some procedures manuals off the other. "Sit down," he said. "Coffee?" To his relief and their health, they both declined.

"How'd it happen?" He glanced from one grim face to the other. Their father was dead, their mother gone since they'd been little. Butt of their pranks or not, he cared more for these two men than anyone else in the world.

"Same as before," Adam said, sounding tired. "Four head this time, tainted feed nearby and an empty bag from the poison left like a warning."

Charlie's pen froze over the pad of paper he'd pulled out to jot down notes. "Warning?" he echoed, switching to full alert.

Adam and Travis exchanged uneasy glances. "Tell him the rest," Travis said, tugging on the end of his mustache like he did when he was nervous.

"Maybe I'll take some coffee after all, if you've

got any more brewed,'' Adam said instead, with a pointed look at Charlie's mug.

''Trust me, you wouldn't want any of this.'' Charlie leaned forward, folding his hands on top of the notepad. ''Now which one of you two clowns is going to fill me in on what's going on?''

Chapter Five

Charlie waited for an answer to his question while Adam sat down in one of the beat-up chairs facing his desk. After a slight hesitation, Travis did the same, steepling his fingers beneath his jaw as though he were praying. Neither man spoke.

"So what makes you think killing the stock is supposed to be some kind of warning?" Charlie spoke in the same tone of voice he'd use on anyone else he suspected of withholding information. "What haven't you told me?"

His oldest brother wasn't an easy man to intimidate, but Charlie tried. He practiced his best gimlet-eyed stare.

Adam's expression was impassive. He crossed one

leg over the other, resting his battered work boot on his knee, and removed his black Resistol. Holding it by the crown, he set it carefully on his bent leg and ran a hand through his shaggy hair. Charlie had seen him use the same gestures countless times in his dealings with suppliers, bankers, buyers and ranch hands.

Charlie resisted the urge to grind his teeth. There were only five years between the two of them, but responsibility had found Adam early and turned him from college student to husband and father in less than a year.

Adam's face revealed nothing, but Charlie refused to be the first to blink or to look away. They were on his turf now, and Adam was no longer dealing with a tagalong baby brother.

"Jeez, are you two going to draw down on each other or what?" Travis's voice exploded in the silence. "Perhaps I should dive for cover."

Charlie knew his middle brother was only trying to lessen the tension. Travis had often played peacemaker.

"You're safe enough for now," Charlie drawled. "If I shoot Adam, then I'll just have to go and suspend myself." He narrowed his gaze. "So one of you clowns better start talking before I change my mind."

"We've had an offer to buy the ranch." Adam's tone was as bland as his face.

Thanks to Adam's management and all their years of hard work, the Running W was the biggest spread in Elbert County and one of the largest in the state that hadn't yet been gobbled up by a conglomerate. The boys had all three been equal partners until a couple of years before when Charlie had sold his interest to the other two so he could buy the club.

Ranching might not be for him, but that wasn't true of his siblings. When their father had dropped dead, Adam quit college to take over. Travis was equally committed, always had been. Charlie couldn't imagine either of them working, living or raising their families anywhere else but Winchester land.

"Who made the offer?" he asked.

Adam frowned and plucked at his hat. "A beef processing conglomerate looking to expand into the supply end of the business."

"You've had offers before." Charlie's jaw was getting tight. His oldest brother's reticence made him feel as though he were grilling a couple of criminals. "So you told them no?"

"Several times." Adam's tone was dry.

"They don't like hearing it," Travis added, his gaze slanting to Adam.

Charlie sat up straighter. Maybe now they were getting somewhere. "Oh? Have they given you any trouble? Made any threats?"

"Naw, of course not," Adam replied. "They're businessmen. They just keep upping the offer." He named a figure that had Charlie's eyes bugging out.

He whistled softly. "You could retire on that, both of you."

"And do what?" Adam shot back. "We're not selling."

Relief washed over Charlie. "I want to look over your correspondence with the outfit that made you the offer. I'll have them checked out."

"But they haven't done anything illegal," Travis protested. "Can you do that?"

"I know a guy who can find out how they do business, that's all," Charlie replied, spreading his hands. "Public records only, I swear."

"Do what you need to," Adam said quietly. "We can't afford to lose many more head."

"So have you thought of anyone with a grudge?" Charlie asked. "Or with anything at all to gain by killing your stock?"

"Mickey Barstow's been hanging around town again," Travis said. "Adam wouldn't rehire him."

Charlie checked the name in his notebook. "Because of his drinking?"

"Yeah." For a moment, Adam studied the band on his hat. It was woven leather. "We gave him several chances, even offered to send him somewhere, but Mickey wasn't ready."

"One time he damn near burned down the hay shed," Travis recalled. "The guy was bad news."

Adam nodded. "Colin Thorpe asked me about him. I had to be honest, but I said that Mickey could have gotten his act together. Colin wasn't inclined to find out."

"So Barstow could be unhappy with you?" Charlie asked.

"One of the boys said Mickey got tanked up down at the Longhorn one night and was shooting off his mouth, but that doesn't prove anything."

"Guess Colin was right not to try him. I'll talk to Barstow." Charlie was writing himself a reminder when the dispatcher stuck his head in the doorway.

"Another burglary last night, boss, over at Malkovich's house on Nugget."

Damn. One more brush fire to put out. "Anyone hurt?" Charlie asked.

"No, sir. They were gone to his sister's in Limon to see her new baby, and they didn't get back till this morning. Found a window broken and some stuff missing, just like the others."

Charlie scratched his chin as he reviewed the file in his mind. For this town, more than two burglaries was a crime wave. "Tell George to call his insurance company and make a list of what's missing. I'll be over later to take a report."

Malkovich lived a couple of blocks down from Robin's house. Maybe Charlie's day was looking up.

"Okay, Sheriff."

After the dispatcher left, Charlie returned his attention to his brothers. "I'll find Barstow and see where his mind is at."

"Sounds like you've got a serial burglar to deal with, too," Travis said. "Is it kids, do you think?"

"Maybe." Someone was taking what they could

sell or fence—CDs, electronics, guns, coins. Booze and cigarettes. A man's gold watch and a flashy ring with a fake stone. "So far we've been lucky, but sooner or later someone's bound to get hurt."

He tapped his pen on the notebook, flipping his attention back to the matter at hand and considering his options. "Have you called Doc Harmon about this last bunch of dead cattle?" he asked.

"Not this time." Adam set his hat back on his head and tugged down the brim. "Cause of death is the same as before, so I didn't see the point."

Charlie pushed back his chair and stood up, needing some fresh air and action. "Well, I'll follow you out there so I can look around." He hated feeling helpless. "Maybe whoever is responsible left something behind."

"Be nice if they dropped a business card," Travis said as Charlie followed him down the hall.

Charlie slapped a hand on his bother's shoulder. "Don't we wish. Meanwhile we've still got Waterloo Days to get through next weekend. There's always a chance some good ol' boy will get blitzed and shoot a tourist."

"What's one tourist, more or less?" Adam quipped.

"Not a big deal unless you happen to run a business that depends on them, like me." Charlie remembered the prospective bartender he needed to interview. How was a man supposed to have a personal life when he juggled two jobs?

He made sure he had his cell phone with him. "John," he said on his way past the dispatcher's desk, "in case anyone needs me, I'm going to the Running W."

Palms damp on the steering wheel, Robin drove slowly through the large parking area in front of the sale barn. She'd come early, but the dirt lot was nearly full of trucks in every conceivable make, model, color and year, except for brand-new. Many had two-tone paint jobs. Some, with their replacement fenders, doors and hoods in different colors, including rust, resembled patchwork quilts. Many of the trucks were dented; all were dusty.

Stock haulers and horse trailers in every size and style waited to be emptied or filled. Pens and corrals contained more animals, all protesting their captivity.

Robin's window was down because of the heat, so the noises assailed her. A rooster crowed and another answered. Horses whinnied, sheep bleated. Someone was playing salsa music. The men and women she drove past, all dressed in jeans and work boots, cowboy hats and baseball caps, stopped what they were doing to watch her. Some smiled. A few waved. One or two frowned.

"Where's the doc?" an old man shouted when she drove by.

"At the dentist." How long until they accepted her?

He frowned and turned away, obviously not happy

with her reply. She pulled into a reserved spot by the door, like Doc Harmon had said. He'd intended to come with her this first time, but a toothache had altered his plans. She'd convinced him she'd be fine, reminding herself now that sale barn work was just part of her job.

It was boring and dirty, but it helped pay the bills. She'd be busy on her own, but she had Doc's list of instructions. The vaccinating, exams, testing and paperwork were nothing she hadn't done before. She would be visible, meet people, get experience—all of which she needed.

She sucked in a steadying breath, got out of the car and opened the back door so she could unload her equipment.

''Need help with anything?'' a male voice asked when she was fishing under the seat for her calculator.

Painfully conscious of the denim-covered view of herself she was presenting to the world, Robin backed out of the car and straightened.

Two tall wiry men in baseball caps and each with a lump of chew distorting one cheek stood looking her over with blatant interest.

''Morning, ma'am,'' said the one with the green John Deere cap.

''You the new vet?'' asked the other, wearing a faded and stained Broncos T-shirt.

''Good morning,'' she replied, introducing herself.

''Got anything that needs carrying inside?'' offered the John Deere cap.

"We can take it for you," added the Broncos shirt, flexing his beefy forearm.

Robin indicated the contents of the back seat. "Those boxes and that bag all go."

"Why don't you boys just cart all that stuff to the exam room next to the sale ring while I consult with Doc Marlowe on some official business?" Charlie Winchester, in khaki and tinted glasses, had managed to sneak up behind Robin. So much for feminine radar.

After being held in his arms the night before, she was jolted by his official appearance and stern expression.

"Sure thing, Sheriff." The John Deere cap tugged at the bill. "Pleased to meet you, ma'am."

Broncos shirt elbowed him in the side. "Call her Doc, you idiot."

While the men each picked up a box, the sheriff cupped Robin's elbow and guided her a few feet away. Despite the morning heat, his callused fingers felt warm against the inside of her arm.

When he released her, she squared her shoulders in an attempt to look professional and wished she'd donned her coveralls before she'd left the house. "Is something wrong?" she asked.

The tinted lenses shielded his gaze, but his mouth quirked into a grin. "How are you?" he asked. "Recovered from your big weekend?"

Was he aware she'd been on call...or referring to

her trip to his club? No doubt the sheriff knew everything that went on in Waterloo.

"I'm just fine," she said briskly, "but I have a lot to do this morning."

"The sale doesn't start for an hour," he drawled. "You could spare me five minutes."

"I have to set up," she protested, glancing around. Her equipment had already disappeared through the open double doors. "I have to—"

"You've got time," he interrupted gently. "Just relax."

"What did you want to talk to me about?" she asked.

To her surprise he seemed to hesitate.

"Is something wrong?" she demanded. Her feelings about him were so mixed. She really needed to sort through them, but right now she wanted to escape.

"No, no, of course not. I didn't mean to alarm you." He scratched the side of his clean-shaven jaw, his gaze intent on hers. "I drove by your house on Saturday afternoon, but you were gone."

"That's right." She had missed him. She ignored a swift jab of disappointment. "I was on a call." They barely knew each other. Did he expect her to sit home? He couldn't be interested in her that way. "Maybe you should have phoned first."

He squared his impressive shoulders. "It wasn't a social visit. I was investigating a burglary a couple of blocks down the street from you and I wondered whether you'd noticed anything suspicious after you got home Friday night.''

"Oh." Omigod. She thought hard for a moment. "No, I can't recall that I did. Any leads?"

"One neighbor saw a couple of tough-looking young guys cruise by earlier that evening. He remembered because they had a load of picnic furniture in the back of their truck and he figured they were looking to sell it. The same pickup, dark blue with a green fender, is parked here today." He shrugged. "I ran the plate, but it's clean."

"Did I move into a high-crime neighborhood?" Robin asked Charlie, who stood with his feet braced apart while he scanned the crowd. Two old men, both stooped from age and hard work, were talking and smoking. A young couple with a baby was looking at a crate full of goats. "Do I need to be worried?"

He patted her shoulder. "Not at all. Just be sure to use that pretty head of yours. Keep your doors and windows locked, okay?"

What he no doubt meant as a gesture of reassurance had the opposite effect on her. His touch made her wary, not of him, but of her own reaction to him.

Pretty head? Trying to give the impression that she received compliments from attractive men all the time, she folded her arms across her chest and returned his smile.

It had been a long time since she'd found a man so appealing. So why couldn't she appreciate Charlie's easy charm and all that hunky male charisma from a safe distance?

Charlie had, with his good-ol'-boy grin and aw-shucks-ma'am flash of dimples, scaled the protective wall she'd spent so much effort erecting. And she would flat-out die if he ever caught a whiff of how she felt.

If she was fortunate, they'd become friends. Buddies, platonic and safe. Maybe they'd hang out together—grab a beer, watch the game. They'd discuss her cases, his job, and maybe he'd tell her about the new woman he was seeing.

The idea stopped Robin's thoughts cold.

Too damn bad that dancing with him, hearing him sing, running into him today made her crave, just for one unguarded moment, something more. Something exciting and dangerous and ultimately, she knew, heartbreaking.

Robin realized Charlie was still watching her with an expectant expression. "So you'll be careful?" he asked.

Careful? She blinked in surprise. Could he read minds, too? "W-with what?" she stammered. Her *heart?* Oh, God!

He removed his sunglasses, hooked them onto his pocket and pinched the bridge of his nose between his thumb and forefinger, as though he was getting a headache—or searching for patience. "Just take sensible precautions, okay? Keep your doors locked, especially at night. Don't hesitate to call 911 if you notice anything, *anything,* suspicious.''

"Oh, sure." *Burglaries.* How could she have forgotten? A bubble of hysteria rose in her throat, but she didn't figure an officer of the law would see humor in the situation. "I hope you apprehend them soon," she added gravely.

She must be losing her mind, trying to keep herself from laughing when she should be worried about crime.

"Oh, we'll catch 'em, don't doubt it. Bottom feeders like that always make some dumb mistake." Charlie dug in his shirt pocket and handed her a card. "Here's the number of my cell. Call me directly if you need anything."

"Sheriff! Sheriff! Come quick!" someone shouted.

Robin and Charlie both turned. One of the older men she'd seen earlier was standing by the side of the building, waving his arms.

"Sheriff Winchester, help, *por favor!* Help us!" There was desperation in the man's voice as he made a sweeping gesture behind him. "They're trying to kill him!"

"José!" Charlie shouted, and then he took off at a dead run.

Robin stood with her mouth hanging open. Kill him? Charlie hadn't taken the time to call in for backup. Some of the stragglers who hadn't gone inside craned their necks, trying to see what was going on, but no one moved to help.

Robin grabbed a big screwdriver with a thick wooden handle from her car and took off after Charlie. His sunglasses flew out of his pocket and fell to the ground, but neither he nor Robin stopped to pick them up.

"What is it, José?" he shouted as he got closer. "What's going on?"

"It's Benito! He's innocent. I swear on the Blessed Virgin!" José stood wringing his hands together and looking back over his shoulder. Tears ran down his leathery cheeks. "You have to stop them."

As she chased Charlie through an empty corral, Robin could hear angry voices over the sounds of the livestock in the nearby pens. José went on ahead.

"Sheriff Charlie is coming!" he shouted. "You will be sorry now!"

When Charlie reached the corner of the building, he slowed to unsnap the flap of his leather holster. Robin came up behind him, breathing hard, and he frowned at her over his shoulder.

"Stay here." His voice was a low-pitched growl.

"You may need backup," she argued.

His gaze dropped to the screwdriver she was holding, white-knuckled, and his face went blank with surprise. "Glory be," he muttered, and then he gestured for her to wait as he stepped out from the side of the building.

Ignoring his silent command, Robin followed him. She was stunned by what she saw.

Two rough-looking wranglers in dirty clothing

were holding a young black-haired man between them while a third man with a dark beard menaced him with fists as big as hams. Blood dripped from the boy's nose, and the whites of his eyes showed like those of a spooked horse as he pleaded with them in a steady stream of Spanish.

"Inocente!" he kept saying. *"Soy inocente!"*

"Make them stop!" José cried. "Benito hasn't done anything wrong!"

"All right, what's going on here?" Charlie demanded in a commanding voice as he walked toward the men.

Robin tightened her grip on the screwdriver just in case, as she watched silently. No one paid her any attention as the men all began talking and shouting at once in a mixture of English and Spanish. One of them gave the boy's arm a vicious twist, making him cry out in pain.

"That's enough!" Charlie's voice cracked like a whip. "Everyone, shut up!"

Silence fell abruptly.

"Glad you're here, Sheriff," replied the man with the beard, even though he didn't look pleased at all. "This is the little punk who broke into my brother's place two weeks ago. We were just about to call you."

"Looks like I saved you a phone call, Burt." Charlie's jaw was rigid with tension, his entire body poised for action. It was a side to him that Robin hadn't even suspected. "Now let him go," he said, "and keep your hands where I can see them."

"He'll run off," one of the men protested.

Charlie stared, eyes narrowed, until the man released his grip on the boy's arm. His buddy did the same.

"You okay?" Charlie pulled a handkerchief from his back pocket and held it out to Benito.

"Sí," the boy replied, *"Gracias."* He wiped the blood from his nose. *"No roto.* Not broken."

Charlie turned his attention back to Burt. "You got any proof he broke into your brother's house?"

"I recognized his truck. It's the same one Harry's neighbor saw that night," the bearded man replied, jabbing his finger at Benito. "Arrest him!"

"The truck's not his," José protested. "Benito borrowed it this morning because his wouldn't start."

"They always stick up for each other," snarled Burt.

"I'll check it out," Charlie told him. "Meanwhile, from the looks of Benito's face, it appears I should haul the three of you vigilantes in for assault."

No one moved, not even Benito. The two men who'd been holding him darted glances at Burt, whose face was flushed as he stared back at Charlie like a cornered grizzly.

Charlie's hand settled onto the butt of his gun. "Don't make it worse."

Burt's shoulders slumped. "I should have figured you'd stick up for him," he sneered. "I knew you'd be too damned much of a bleeding heart to make a decent sheriff.''

"Good to know you didn't vote for me, Burt," Charlie drawled. "Makes me like you even less than I did before." His gaze shifted. "Benito, you want to press charges against these clowns?''

"No, Señor Charlie." He lowered the handkerchief from his nose, already starting to swell, and shook his head.

Charlie's eyes narrowed. "You sure?''

Benito's response was a blur of Spanish.

"If you're not going to arrest him," José translated, "he just wants to go home and put ice on his nose so he can go to work.''

Robin could see Charlie's frustration. "We need to talk so I can fill out a report." He tapped his badge and addressed Benito directly. "Come to my office later. Don't worry about working tonight. Carlos can fill in for you.''

"What are you talking about?" Burt protested angrily as the boy and the old man walked away. "Aren't you taking him in?''

"Benito's a dishwasher at my club," Charlie explained. "I know where to find him.''

"Who's she?" Burt jerked his head in Robin's direction as though he'd noticed her for the first time. "New lady friend?" He managed to make the term sound like an insult.

Apparently his companions were content to let him do the talking for all three of them. They stood with their heads down and their thumbs hooked into their belts, both of them kicking at the dirt with the toes of their boots like naughty children waiting to be scolded.

Charlie glanced at Robin as though he'd forgotten all about her. "Lady friend?" he echoed with a glance at her screwdriver and a quirk of his mouth that could have been a grin. "Naw, she's my newest deputy, and she's mean as a snake."

A cheer from the sale barn had snapped Robin back to reality and reminded her that she was here for a reason and it wasn't playing cops and robbers. After she'd made sure that Charlie had things under control, she'd torn back around the building to a side door.

Relief washed over her when she saw that no one was waiting for her services. After she donned a pair of coveralls to keep her clothing reasonably clean, she organized her testing and vaccinating equipment with hands that shook.

How unbelievable that it was still morning! So much had happened. Her heart was thudding in delayed reaction to the scene she and Charlie had interrupted.

What if he hadn't been here to stop those men? She hated bullies. They needed to be taught a lesson. What a shame that Benito had been too scared to press charges, but perhaps Charlie would be able to change his mind at the station this afternoon. She hoped so!

Robin was standing with her hands on her hips, reviewing her duties, when she heard footsteps behind her. Taking a deep breath, she turned around, prepared to begin her duties.

"You okay?" Charlie was studying her as he removed his hat and wiped his forehead with his other sleeve.

"Of course," she replied, ignoring the surge of awareness she seemed unable to control. It had been a stressful morning, that was all. "Did you find out anything else after I left?"

He shook his head. "Bunch of jerks."

"Men like that deserve to be in jail," she said with a shudder.

"I agree." He stared down at the table. "I really hate days like today," he muttered.

"Why?" she demanded. "Benito could have been badly hurt if you hadn't stopped those men."

He tapped the star on his chest with his finger. "If I hadn't taken an oath to uphold the law, I could have shown Burt what a beating feels like from the receiving end." A muscle jumped in Charlie's cheek, and his tone was grim. "Sometimes wearing a badge has its drawbacks."

"Do you think there's a chance the boy might be guilty?" she asked.

He shook his head. "No way. I know the family. I'll look into it, of course, but compared to Benito's mama, Burt's a pussycat." He took out his notebook and flipped it open. "I'm going to run down the owner of the pickup Bennie borrowed, though. It's quite a coincidence that it was spotted at two crime scenes, and I just don't believe in coincidences."

Robin laced her fingers together in front of her. "I hope you'll keep me informed, as much as you can."

"Sure thing," he replied. "And I wanted to thank you for watching my back the way you did, too."

She glanced down at her hands. "I didn't do anything."

"But you would have, wouldn't you?" He lifted her chin up with his finger so their gazes met. "That's what the screwdriver was for."

She pulled away nervously. "I guess."

"Well, I have to say that it was quick thinking on your part and I appreciate it. If you ever want a new career, I'll consider taking you on as a deputy." His eyes crinkled at the outer corners when he smiled, his scrutiny making her self-conscious.

"Did you find your sunglasses?" she asked, glad to be able to shift the focus of their conversation away from herself. "I saw them fall out of your pocket when you ran through the parking lot, but I didn't take the time to pick them up."

He patted his shirt pocket. "Damn. I suppose someone's run over them by now, but I'll look on my way out."

Robin had never been good at clever conversation or lighthearted flirting. Silently she waited for him to go.

"One more thing before I let you get to work," he

said. "Would you like to go riding with me one afternoon this week? I keep a couple of saddle horses at my brothers' spread."

The invitation caught her totally off guard. "I don't know what my hours are yet."

He shrugged. "We'll go after you get off work. Waterloo Days starts on Friday, so I'll be on duty all weekend. Why don't you ask Doc about Thursday?"

For once Robin was torn between what was sensible and what she wanted. "I guess I could talk to him," she replied hesitantly. "But I haven't ridden in a long time."

His grin widened. "We'll find you an old nag. The practice will be good for you." He glanced around. The sale was getting underway. "I'll call you."

Before she could reply, one of the officials came up. Charlie greeted him and turned back to Robin.

"Thanks again for the help, Doc," he said with a wink.

Chapter Six

"Riding a horse is like riding a bicycle," Charlie told Robin as they drove down the road that ran along Winchester property. "You don't forget."

She'd been waiting for him on the porch of her rental house wearing new Western boots, old jeans and an oversize plaid shirt. The idea that she'd bought a pair of boots to go riding with him gave his ego a nice little stroke.

Now smooth jazz played on the stereo, the temperature was pleasant, and they had several hours of daylight left. Life didn't get much better, he thought as he sucked in a deep breath of fresh, clean air.

"That may be so, but it's truly been longer than I care to remember since I've been on horseback,"

Robin replied, fiddling with a thin silver ring on her right hand. It was the only jewelry she wore, and the single pink stone was probably her birthstone. "Maybe this wasn't such a good idea."

Charlie reached over to cover her hand with his. "Trust me, it's a great idea," he corrected her gently. Darned if he was going to let her change her mind now that he'd gotten her all to himself for a couple of hours.

He clenched his teeth. "You don't have to ride if you really don't want to, but I think you'll have fun."

"Do you promise to give me a nice, gentle, slow horse?" she asked, neither pulling away from his touch nor turning over her hand to clasp his.

He raised his eyebrows as he grabbed the gearshift and slowed for the turn through the ranch's front gates. "Gentle?" he echoed as she looked out her side window. "Well, most of them are only green broke, but we can tie a pillow to your butt in case you get thrown, okay? That way the landing won't hurt so much."

Her head snapped around, her dark eyes wide with alarm. When she saw his grin, she scowled and slapped at his forearm.

"Very funny! With that line, I'll bet you don't get many girls to go riding with you."

He winked as he drove across the cattle guard, the familiar feeling of coming home tugging at him. "Not many greenhorns," he replied.

Even without cosmetics, her lashes were thick, her

naked lips pink and velvety. Thinking about the possibility of tasting that mouth made his own water with anticipation. He suspected letting her see how attracted he was would make her bolt like a wild hare. Local girls had been chasing him down since grade school, so Robin's reserve was a challenge. More than that, he liked her.

"So you grew up here on the ranch?" she asked as he turned down the road that ran past his brothers' houses to the stables. He didn't figure on riding too long this first time, just far enough for a little privacy.

"That's right," he said. "When I bought the club, I moved to town."

"Do your parents still live around here?" she asked, looking out the window.

Since everyone in Elbert County knew the story, her innocent question caught him off guard, causing a dull ache he thought he'd put behind him.

"Dad died when I was in high school," he said. The truck bounced across some wheel ruts and raised a cloud of dust, so he eased back on the gas pedal and loosened his grip on the wheel. "I don't know about my mother." After all this time, he still stumbled on that word, *mother,* but calling her anything else would only invite more questions—and thinking of appropriate answers would give the woman an importance she'd tossed away when she'd left.

Robin looked surprised, but she didn't ask anything else. "I'm sorry," she said instead. "My parents died when I was fourteen. We never really get over it, do we?''

His initial relief that she'd changed the subject was wiped away by dismay. ''Both of them? My God, that's awful. I'm sorry.''

They passed Travis's house, which Charlie had shared before Travis married Rory. The yard and porch were empty, and Rory's van was gone.

''Pretty flowers,'' Robin said.

Charlie glanced at Rory's customary collection of hanging baskets and wildly blooming pots in a riot of brilliant colors. ''They belong to my singing sister-in-law,'' he explained. ''No pastels for Rory.''

He cleared his throat and sneaked a glance at Robin's profile. ''Does it bother you to talk about your parents?'' Like it did him?

''Not so much. They were in a car accident.'' She looked down at her hands. ''The only good thing about it was that they went together. Neither had to live without the other.'' The sadness in her voice tore at him.

Way to go, Winchester. What a fun date.

''Were you left all alone?'' he asked, unable to stop himself from asking. ''No one else?''

She shook her head. ''No, no family at all except my father's older sister. She was a widow with a grown son, so I didn't think she would want me, but she did. When the time came, she made sure I went to college.''

They drove past Adam's house, all glass and river

rock. A plastic basketball hoop and a trike with a huge front wheel had been left in the driveway. What a change from the bleakness of the place after Adam's first wife left, before Emily had come along and reformed him.

"Your aunt must be proud of you," Charlie said to Robin. They had something in common, losing parents early, but unlike Robin, he'd had two brothers to lean on. He couldn't imagine being an only child.

Her lips trembled before she pressed them together and ducked her head. "Aunt Dot had a bad heart. She'd encouraged me to try for veterinary school, but she passed away while I was still in college."

Once again he reached over to cover her hand with his. This time he gave it a hard squeeze. To his surprise and delight, she put her free hand on top of his and patted it twice. The gesture was hardly romantic, but it warmed him.

"I think it's time to lighten up a little, don't you?" he asked. "How big a pillow do you think you'll need to cushion your fall?"

In the center aisle of the stable, Charlie cross-tied the first of their two mounts, a handsome bay gelding, and inspected all four hooves. Watching him clean them with a pick, Robin wiggled her toes in her new Western boots. She'd bought them especially for today and she'd worried they might hurt her feet, but the soft leather was surprisingly comfortable. The riding heels made her feel tall.

"Zodiac is a quarter horse," Charlie explained as he rubbed the white spot on the bay's forehead. "He was trained as a cutting horse and he's quick as a cat, but he's as calm as an old hound."

As Charlie worked, he explained each step of the process to Robin. He set the pad on Zodiac's wide back, positioned the saddle, unfolded the various straps and belts and tightened the girth.

Robin was more interested in watching him work, gazing at the easy shift of muscles beneath his striped shirt and listening to the way his voice rose and fell, than in actually paying much attention to what he said. It wasn't as though riding together, or doing anything together for that matter, was going to become a habit, she told herself between staring and drooling. Might as well soak him in while she had the chance.

And Robin was a woman who prided herself on keeping her distance, she mused with a disbelieving shake of her head. He checked the stirrups, and she checked out his compact rear in worn denim. Ah, well. She'd return to her ivory tower soon enough, whenever Charlie found the novelty of spending time with a plain, quiet, inhibited female wearing off.

Robin had no idea why he'd invited her along today. Maybe he was just being friendly, or maybe it was part of some welcome-to-Waterloo initiation. Or perhaps—God forbid—he was doing Doc Harmon a favor. She slapped the cap she'd brought against her thigh.

Give the spinster a thrill.

That idea stopped her cold for about a second and a half before she dismissed it. The day was too pleasant, the sky outside was too blue and the breeze too fresh for her to waste her time trying to decipher his motives. For now she'd ignore the *why* of it and concentrate on the *what* instead.

Charlie led Zodiac away, humming a vaguely familiar melody as he replaced the muscular bay with a smaller gray horse. Zodiac snorted, and the gray swished her tail flirtatiously, prancing sideways on impossibly delicate legs.

Zodiac ignored the teasing. Waste of time, Robin thought with a smirk.

She went back to watching the sheriff hitch the mare in place. Charlie was good to look at from every angle, his voice made her pulse race, and he carried a gun in case she needed protection. What more could a woman want in a man?

"Your turn."

She blinked, dragging her gaze back to his face. "Huh?"

"You can saddle Pansy," he invited, stepping back. "I'll supervise."

Clueless, Robin stared with dismay at the remaining saddle and the pile of tack.

"Pansy?" she echoed, arching her brows in the hope of diverting his attention.

His cheeks reddened, which managed to increase

his appeal, as he glanced at the pretty gray mare and scratching his tanned throat.

"Uh, an old girlfriend helped to foal Pansy, so it seemed fair at the time for her to choose the name." He shrugged, grinning. "Afterward, I wasn't so sure."

Of course he had old girlfriends, dozens, maybe even hundreds. "That explanation must have been a big hit around the campfire," she guessed, returning his smile.

He rolled his eyes. "Oh, yeah." Lightly he stroked the mare's back. "She's a sweetheart, though, with a trot as smooth as a clarinet solo. I think you'll like her."

Robin couldn't resist. "I'm guessing you're referring to the horse and not the ex-girlfriend?" As soon as the words were out, she wished she could call them back. Perhaps she'd assumed too much. Maybe the girlfriend wasn't an ex. What did Robin really know about Charlie's personal life?

Not much.

Kidding and flirtatious banter weren't things she had a lot of practice with, so she wanted to kick herself when Charlie gave her a startled glance. Then he slapped his thigh, threw back his head and roared with laughter while Pansy's ears twitched.

Robin's face burned hotter as she tried, and failed, to curb a chuckle of her own. Soon she and Charlie were both laughing out loud. His eyes still danced with amusement when he grabbed her shoulders and planted a smacking kiss on her cheek. She barely had time to stiffen before he let her go again.

He must have noticed, because his smile faded. "I'm not seeing anyone else, if that's what you're asking," he said quietly. "How about you? Any boyfriends back in Chicago I should be concerned with?"

For a moment, her tongue refused to work properly. Her cheek still tingled from the too-brief brand of his mouth. Her shoulders still bore the firm, heated imprint of his hands. Her heart went all fluttery at the revelation that he was unattached.

"Um, no," she managed, her gaze darting everywhere but at him as she answered his question. "No boyfriends."

Pansy stamped her foot, no doubt impatient to get going. Zodiac blew out a breath and shook his head, bridle jingling.

Charlie hadn't moved. He startled Robin by tucking a finger under her chin and lifting her head so she had no choice but to meet his gaze. "How about exes?" he murmured. "Maybe someone who's hurt you?" So he'd noticed the way she'd frozen up.

Brian's image popped into her head, handsome and charming. Unwelcome. Oh, yes, he'd hurt her, but not in the way Charlie meant. She shivered, wrapping her arms around her middle to ward off the sudden chill.

"Cold?" Charlie asked, clearly puzzled.

Robin shook her head. "It's really quite pleasant out, not as hot as yesterday." Her voice sounded odd, even to her own ears, so she looked pointedly at Pansy. "Shouldn't we get this show on the road?"

"Sure thing." He finished saddling the mare. At least Robin had succeeded in distracting him from having her do the job herself.

As soon as both horses were ready, Charlie slapped on his hat and led them outside, his hands moving by rote as his mind mulled over what Robin had told him, especially the way she'd overreacted to his question about ex-boyfriends.

She was a complicated woman, more so than he'd first thought, even though he'd felt a tug of interest from the start. The sense of humor she'd shown today intrigued him, but that hint of vulnerability made him want to comfort her. To protect her, even from himself if necessary.

Something much more recent than the loss of her parents, *someone,* had bruised her heart. His fist tightened on the reins. Some people viewed him as a playboy, a flirt, but he tried hard never to be thoughtless or selfish.

He gave Robin a reassuring smile, ready to boost her into the saddle.

"You remember more about riding than you let on," he said after she'd mounted without his assistance.

She gathered up the reins and grinned down at him, cheeks flushed, as he adjusted her stirrups. When he was done, Pansy shifted unexpectedly, but Robin didn't grab the horn or squeal with fright. Her body adapted to the movement easily, automatically.

She leaned down and patted Pansy's neck. "It's coming back."

They walked their horses to the pasture gate while he filled her in on his interview with Benito.

"I had no reason to hold him," Charlie concluded, "and no luck changing his mind about pressing assault charges against those other creeps."

"He was lucky you were willing to jump in with no idea of what you'd be facing," she replied.

"Makes me sound pretty dumb."

"No, you were very brave," she argued, making him feel good.

"You were the brave one," he told her as he bent down to open the gate. "It's my job, after all, but I'll never forget the sight of you waving that screwdriver. Talk about a rush. You got my hormones jumping."

"I didn't *wave* it," she exclaimed as they rode through the opening. She waited while he fastened the gate shut. "My God, you could have been facing darned near anything behind that building. I just wanted to be prepared."

"Well, thanks again." He shook his head, remembering his stunned surprise that she'd followed him. What a woman.

"So tough broads get to you?" she asked, cocking her head and giving him a considering look. "Biker chicks? Women wrestlers?"

"Sure," he bantered back. "Tight leather always

works. Got any tattoos?'' He fanned himself with one hand. ''How about piercings? Man, the idea of that makes me feel faint.''

''Yeah, the idea of having it done,'' she shot back.

He laughed and then he indicated the pasture ahead with a questioning gesture. ''Feel like picking up the pace a little?''

To his delight, she urged Pansy into a trot.

''She's like a rocking chair!'' Robin shouted, sitting easy in the saddle.

Charlie could feel Zodiac's frustration as the bay tossed his head. His muscles were bunched, his gate stiff. The gelding had been neglected, and he needed a good run. Charlie looked at Robin expectantly. ''Ready for more?''

By the time they reached the next gate, Robin's confidence had soared. As a child going through the typical horse-crazy stage, she'd taken lessons for two summers and gone to riding camp. She hadn't thought about it for a long time, but now the enjoyment came flooding back.

''How are you doing?'' Charlie asked when they'd both slowed at the fence. ''Okay?''

''Wonderful!'' She tossed back her head so she had to grab at her cap or lose it. Pansy pranced beneath her, as if she, too, was enjoying the outing. ''I don't know how I stayed off horses for as long as I did.''

''You're welcome to come out and ride anytime,''

Charlie said as he fiddled with the gate and finally dismounted. "Pansy could use the exercise."

Head down, Robin led his horse through the opening. "Thanks," she mumbled, embarrassed that he might think she'd been hinting.

After he'd closed the stubborn gate again, he mounted in a motion so fluid that it was poetic.

"There's almost always someone around to help you, but you probably shouldn't ride alone for now." He grinned, dispelling her discomfort as he leaned closer. "Just give me a call." His voice was husky. "I'll take you riding anytime you want."

The laughter in his eyes, the flash of dimples, turned the cheesy come-on into a shared joke.

"That's terrible! Are you always such a flirt?" she demanded, taking off her cap to bat him on the shoulder.

His horse sidestepped. "What do you classify as always?" Charlie asked.

"I should report you to the sheriff. I hear he's a real straight arrow when it comes to harassment of any kind."

Charlie glanced over his shoulder as Zodiac moved ahead. "There was a rumor going around that he's got a real weakness for petite women with short hair and dark eyes."

Any ability she might have for flirtatious banter evaporated as suddenly as a raindrop on a griddle. Had he only been kidding about finding her attractive?

Apparently he didn't expect an answer, because he urged the bay forward.

"Let's take a break over by that rise," he suggested as they rode side by side. "We can stretch our legs and rest the horses."

"Okay." She was so busy attempting to analyze her reaction to him that she didn't say anything more. For a few moments they rode silently except for the pleasant creaking of saddle leather, the jangle of the bridles and the sound of their horses' hoofbeats.

Robin was about to break the silence with a comment on the peace out here in the wide-open spaces when she happened to look down.

There were splashes of color among the grasses that she'd been too distracted to notice until now.

Wildflowers!

"Oh, how pretty," she exclaimed, leaning down to examine the scattering of blooms. "What are they?"

Charlie leaned over, too. "Well, let me see," he muttered. "The purple is clover, but you probably already knew that. The little yellow ones are some kind of violet, I think, and the big ones with the dark centers are black-eyed Susans."

"I see some Johnny jump-ups!" Robin exclaimed excitedly as she pointed. "What do you call them here?"

"Same thing," he replied. "And there's vetch and flax around here, too." He stood in his stirrups. "There are even more that flower in the spring."

"I'm surprised you know the names," she replied,

sneaking glances at his profile. On horseback, he could have ridden through a time portal from a hundred years before, his rugged appeal making her mouth go dry.

As if he'd read her mind, he pulled a bottle of water from his saddle bag and offered it to her.

"Thirsty?"

"Thanks." Popping the top, Robin tipped back her head and swallowed. When she handed the bottle back, he was looking at her with a bemused expression.

"What?" she asked warily.

"Uh, nothing." He took a drink and she watched the muscles of his throat work as he swallowed.

Some things didn't change over time. He made her feel lightheaded.

"You asked about the flower names," he said when he'd tucked away the bottle. "I only know the common ones. Some plants, like lupine, can be toxic to the cattle, so we're always watching for them."

Their horses had reached the small rise he'd indicated earlier. When she dismounted, Robin was startled to find that her legs were shaky.

"Take a hot bath tonight," Charlie suggested, watching her take a few tentative steps. "Otherwise your muscles might be sore in the morning."

Robin looked around. Obviously there was nowhere to tether Pansy. "Should I just hang onto her reins so she doesn't run off?"

"Haven't you watched any Westerns?" Charlie

asked, hands on hips. "Winchester horses are all trained to be ground tied. If you drop her reins, she won't stray."

"Really?" She wasn't sure if he was joshing her or not, but she didn't figure he'd risk walking back.

Instead of answering, he let go of Zodiac's reins. The horse stood quietly while Charlie got the water and a package of cookies. "Let's sit down for a few minutes." He took Robin's hand in his and gave it a tug, leading her to a patch of grass.

Carefully she sat down next to him.

"Stiff?" he asked.

She wasn't about to admit that he made her nervous. "A little bit."

He cocked one brow. "I could massage your muscles." He set the water and the cookies between them. Holding up his hands up, he flexed them. "I'm very talented."

The idea of him touching her that way stirred up a mixture of feelings in Robin, but his exaggerated leer put her at ease. "Thanks, but I'll take your word on that," she said.

He shrugged. "Just keep it in mind." Drawing up one knee, he rested his arm on it.

He was fun to be with, she decided as she lay back on the warm grass and tucked her hands under her head. The sun was dropping low in the sky, but she wasn't the least bit chilled. A couple of birds flew overhead, one squawking as if telling the other to wait up.

Robin sighed and closed her eyes. Relaxation seeped through her like warm honey, turning her boneless with pleasure and making her moan with enjoyment. After a moment, a shadow blocked out the brightness beyond her closed lids. Startled, she opened her eyes to see Charlie leaning over her, staring intently at her mouth.

Alarm surged through her like an electric current. With a squeak of fright, she shoved hard at his shoulders and rolled away. She scrambled to her hands and knees, but before she could stand, Charlie's voice cut through her panic.

"Easy, easy. Robin, honey, it's okay," he said in a low, steady voice. "I won't hurt you. I'd never hurt you."

Her panic began to subside, letting her breathe. She hung her head.

"Take it easy." Slowly he extended his hand. "I'm sorry, baby. I'm so sorry I startled you." His fingers brushed the skin of her forearm and then he merely waited.

She drew in a deeper breath, tears of humiliation burning her eyes, and sat back down on the grass. She wanted to hide her face behind her hands. "No," she whispered instead, "I'm the one who's sorry. I overreacted."

After a moment he touched her shoulder. "You okay?"

She nodded. "Can we go back now?" Her voice

sounded small to her ears, shaky, just the way she felt.

"Sure thing. Come on." He got to his feet and extended his hand. Without looking at his face, she took it and let him pull her up. As she stood with her head bowed, wishing the ground would open up so she could disappear, he pulled out a handkerchief and extended it.

She wiped at her eyes and handed it back. Finally she had no choice but to raise her head. "I'm sorry," she said again.

He shook his head, shushing her with a finger pressed gently to her lips. "No, no. It was my fault. I sneaked up on you." He shifted his finger to her cheek, stroking it with a feather light touch. "Guess my technique needs work. It's rustier than I thought." He dropped his hand and sighed. "Never had a girl scream before, I don't think."

There was humor and understanding in his tone. Sympathy.

"I didn't scream," Robin argued, feeling slightly less stupid. If he could joke about it, perhaps he wasn't too disgusted with her.

"Scared the horses."

She looked at Pansy and Zodiac, neither of whom were paying the slightest attention. In truth, they seemed to be dozing. "I don't think so."

"Scared me, though," he muttered under his breath, his petulant tone bringing a reluctant smile to her lips.

"Ohh, poor boy," she cooed, patting his cheek with the flat of her free hand.

He covered it with his own, holding her palm to the side of his face. She had no choice but to return his gaze, her nervousness returning as she searched his brown eyes for pity or scorn. If he felt either, he hid it well.

"So," he said softly as he released her and rested both big hands lightly on her shoulders. "Do you feel like telling me what just happened back there?"

She chewed at her lip. "Can I just say that it wasn't your fault—nothing you did—and leave the rest for some other time?"

He squeezed her shoulders and then he dropped his hands. "Sure thing."

She couldn't leave it, not when she heard the disappointment in his voice. He'd blame himself. Without thinking she reached up and caught his face in her hands. "Wait."

He froze. Their gazes locked. Despite the extra few inches the new boots gave her, she was still too short, so she urged him closer.

"You don't have to do this." His voice was husky.

"Please," she murmured, staring into his eyes, watching his pupils expand with awareness. She braced herself, but he didn't swoop. Didn't lunge.

He drifted down to her, arms at his sides. Slowly, as she slid her hands to his neck and then to his shoulders, he touched his mouth to hers, pressing gently, and sipped.

Chapter Seven

It was to reassure Robin and to satisfy his own curiosity that Charlie kissed her, he told himself as he leaned down. His last rational thought, touching her lips, was that he'd been right about them. They were soft and warm. His mistake was in assuming just a taste would be enough.

Reaction seeped into him, warm as sunlight, gentle as a breath. It teased him into thinking he was in control. Her hands slid over his chest, fingers flexing against the fabric of his shirt. Stroking him.

Her mouth heated—warm to hot. Cozy to sizzling. The tip of her tongue traced a sly path from one corner of his upper lip to the other. He trembled—letting her lead—swallowed a groan of dismay when she lifted her mouth and then stifled a grateful sigh as she angled her head and came back for more.

She nibbled at his lips, and his knees turned to water. He barely resisted the urge to grab, to dive in and gobble her up. Instead, shaking with the effort, he let her explore. Test and tease him. Until heat turned to fire and want turned to need. And control wavered.

Before it could shatter around them, he cupped her face in hands that trembled and peeled his mouth off hers.

Her eyes popped open, pupils big enough, black enough, to drown in. For a moment she and Charlie stared at each other, gasping.

The strength of his reaction unnerved him as he searched her face for signs of fear, but saw instead a mix of confusion and, perhaps, desire.

Timid temptress or skilled minx?

She stepped back, and he dropped his hands. At least she wasn't swinging a slap at him. That was something.

"Well," he meant to say, but croaked out instead. He swallowed hard and tried again. "You pack a hell of a punch," he blurted.

Aw, hell. Feeling like a green kid after his first kiss, Charlie scrubbed a hand over his face. He'd probably only made things worse by letting what had started as a friendly peck go up in flames.

The realization hit him with the force of a back-handed blow that he'd gone a lot *further* with women on occasion and been affected a lot *less*.

Robin blinked those big eyes, cute as a baby owl, and linked her fingers together while she studied him. Head tilted to the side. Probably waiting for him to fall on her like a starved dog and devour her.

"You don't have to pretend to be blown away," she finally said with a sniff.

Pretend? If his tongue hung out any farther, he'd be standing on it.

"Sweetheart," he said, "I've had throws from wild bulls that affected me less than that kiss."

Doubt shadowed her eyes and spiked her brows. "Really? You aren't just saying that?" Her lips, still moist, trembled, corners lifting.

Charlie nodded as his raging hormones finally cooled and his brain function stumbled toward normal. What she needed, he saw with a pang, was reassurance that she'd swayed him. Who the hell had stripped away her confidence in herself as a woman and left her so vulnerable? So unsure of her charms?

This wasn't the time for swaggering male bravado or protecting his own ego. "Yeah," he agreed with a crooked smile. "Really. At least a twelve on that one-to-ten scale."

A smile, tentative at first, and then stronger, curved her mouth. Her cheeks bloomed with color and her eyelashes fluttered.

She looked…immensely pleased with herself.

Unable to resist, Charlie grabbed her hand and

bowed over it. After he'd pressed his lips to the soft skin, he turned her hand over and ran his tongue across her palm. Her fingers curled.

"Just checking," he muttered.

"On what?" she asked as he led her toward the horses.

"That I wasn't the only one affected by that kiss."

"Oh," she said softly, blush deepening, but she didn't elaborate.

It was enough for now.

"Since I don't suppose you'd be willing to roll around on the ground with me and I didn't think to bring a bedroll, we might as well head back," he said. Watching her reaction to his teasing was quickly becoming his second favorite activity.

"I've got an inflatable mattress in my purse," she replied, eyes dancing with mischief, but then she snapped her fingers. "Oh, darn. I left it in your pickup."

He risked sneaking an arm around her shoulders. "There's always an empty stall in the horse barn," he whispered into her ear. "An inflatable mattress you say?"

Robin waved at the departing red pickup one last time and then she floated up her side porch steps, dropping her keys twice before she managed to focus on the door lock in front of her. Feeling more than a little tipsy, with nothing stronger on her breath but water and nothing in her mind but Charlie, she pressed her fingers to her sensitized lips, still tingling from his brief parting kiss, and swallowed another giggle.

No point in giving her landlady the impression she'd been hitting the bottle too hard. Knowing Mae, she'd be over to help with a pot of black coffee. Or an ice bag and a pitcher of Bloody Marys for tomorrow morning.

The image made Robin giggle again as she finally got the door open and sneaked a glance over her shoulder. There was no sign that her neighbors were home, so they'd probably gone to bingo down at the church.

Charlie had promised Robin a pizza after they'd turned out the horses, but an urgent call on his cell phone made him scowl and change their plans.

''Rain check?'' he'd asked after he'd pulled up at the end of her driveway and apologized for not seeing her right to her door. She'd agreed, and he had jumped out of the truck to open her door before she could stop him.

He'd left her with a quick, hard kiss and a promise to call. Would he lie about that when he must know they'd run into each other constantly? She guessed she'd find out.

Now she hummed softly as she tugged off her fancy new boots and then her socks. Wiggling her toes against the ancient vinyl floor, she selected a dinner from the freezer, a beef fajita rice bowl, and popped it into the microwave she'd owned since college.

Knowing Charlie had been in a hurry to meet his deputy at the station had helped Robin withstand the urgent desire to deepen that last kiss. Now the mental picture of herself, grabbing him by the ears and standing on tiptoe to reach his mouth while she probably knocked off his hat in the process, kept her smiling as she fished mismatched silverware from the drawer. She danced across the kitchen to the table.

Robin never giggled. Nor did she ever make moves on men, especially not hunks like Charlie. And she certainly didn't fall for a date's careless promise to call again.

Never.

She must be under the influence of something in the air blowing down from the Rockies, she thought, pouring a diet cola into a tall glass. The bell on the microwave dinged, so she retrieved the rice bowl with a wistful sigh and an experimental sniff. Charlie and pizza sounded way more appealing than the rice bowl smelled.

Before she sat down, she retrieved the mail she'd tossed aside earlier. When she glanced in the oval wall mirror she'd found at a thrift store in Urbana, her reflection stunned her.

The flaws in the mirror's silvered back failed to detract from the attractive pink flush of her cheeks. Her brown eyes brimmed with smiles and secrets. Her hair, still wind tossed from the ride, stuck up in rather trendy spikes.

She turned her head from one side to the other, studying her image. Below the short haircut, her earlobes looked awfully naked. Maybe she'd get them pierced so she could wear Aunt Dot's garnet studs.

She drew her mouth into an experimental moue. Her lips were full enough and their shape was okay, but they looked awfully pale. Perhaps she'd have to break down and invest in some gloss.

She plopped down at the table, curling her toes against the texture of the oval rag rug beneath it, and pulled in her chair. Flipping through the envelopes and junk mail, she set aside a newsletter from the University of Illinois Alumni Association.

She scooped up a forkful of rice and sauce. Not bad, for frozen fodder. As she chewed, she skimmed the contents of the flyer until one name snagged her attention.

Brian.

Her stomach clenched. Damn. She tried without success to drag her gaze away from the paragraph below his name.

"…in partnership with his father at a successful Chicago veterinary practice, married to the daughter of a prominent local attorney…" trumpeted the item.

Robin set the newsletter aside with a hand that shook and swallowed hard against the bile rising in her throat. Trembling all over, she stared at the table. The dinner that had seemed fine just moments before, now had all the appeal of last week's garbage. Needing to do something, anything, she got to her feet, tipping her chair over, and dumped the food into the can beneath the counter. Then she turned around, hand pressed to her stomach, and leaned over the sink.

Eyes closed, hands braced, she waited for the nausea to pass. When it did, she straightened and sucked in a long, slow breath.

She'd bet a month's pay that Brian hadn't raped his trophy wife on *their* first date, the way he'd raped Robin.

Before she could push back the painful memories that threatened to fill her mind like toxic fumes, the phone on the kitchen wall rang, startling her.

She didn't feel like talking to anyone, not right now, so she let the phone ring two more times until her answering machine took over and played its brief message.

"Robin, are you there?" asked a familiar voice. "I'm sorry to bother you at home, but something's come up. I need you to call me back as soon as you get this."

Even though she wasn't technically on duty tonight, she couldn't ignore a message from her boss. With a sigh, she grabbed the receiver.

Moments later she was reading back to Doc the directions she'd jotted down on the pad she kept on the counter. "No problem," she insisted. "I'm leaving right now, so you can tell Mr. Bassett I'm on my way.''

"You did right to call me," Charlie told his deputy, Samuel Redd. "What have you got?"

Samuel flipped open his notebook. "Like I told you on the phone, I was calling pawnshops with the list of stuff that's missing in those burglaries," he replied, frowning over his notes. "I just got a hit on some binoculars and a man's watch that sound like they could be the ones we're looking for."

Charlie parked his butt on the corner of his desk and idly swung one leg back and forth. He'd much rather be eating pizza with Robin, but this was a case he needed to solve before someone got hurt.

"Which pawnshop?" he asked.

"Hottinger's over in Castle Rock. I'd left the owner a message, and he just got back to me."

Charlie nodded. "I'm familiar with the shop and with him. Not a bad guy. So what makes you think he's got the right goods?"

Samuel fiddled with the silver stud in his ear, struggling without success to stifle a smug grin. "Engraving on the back of the watch just happens to match the description of the one on the list, FJB in block letters."

Charlie perked up like a hound dog on a fresh scent. "That's a good indication," he said dryly. "Was he able to give you anything on who brought them in?"

Samuel's smile widened, creasing his tanned cheeks and nearly squeezing his black eyes shut. Samuel was a Ute who'd grown up on the reservation before coming to Waterloo a decade before. "Three guys," he said.

"And?" Charlie prompted. He was getting a little impatient, seeing how he could have been sharing pizza, and perhaps more, with Robin at this very moment.

Charlie kept his voice even, his expression bland. "How about you cut to the chase and give me the rest of what you've got before I grab you by the throat and shake it out of you."

Samuel sobered abruptly. "Okay, Sheriff. Sure thing." He went on to describe three losers Charlie had dealt with very, very recently.

When Samuel was done, Charlie got to his feet. "Good police work." He slapped Samuel on the shoulder. "Let me get changed and then we'll go talk to them." It was for situations like this that he kept a spare uniform in his office closet. "I'm curious about where Burt's going to say he was, the night his brother's house was getting broken into."

Samuel bobbed his head. "Thanks, boss." For some reason he didn't look very pleased with himself.

"Something else?" Charlie asked.

Everyone knew that a big part of the reason Samuel had been hired in the first place was that the former sheriff was under pressure to do so. Since then, Samuel had taken a long list of law enforcement courses, paying for them out of his pocket when the department couldn't afford them.

Most important, he had a nose for police work.

"Are you taking over?" he asked quietly.

Charlie grinned. "You cracked it, you follow up, okay? I'm just going along for backup."

Just the way Robin had followed Charlie behind the sale barn with a screwdriver clenched in one hand, he thought. She'd been ready to face who-knew-what, but today she'd turned pale when he'd leaned over to kiss her. What a puzzle. Before his mind could go farther down that road, he yanked it back to the present.

"I appreciate it," Samuel said gruffly. "And I never thanked you for keeping me on when you took over. You didn't have to do that."

No point in letting things get all mushy, right before they went out to chase bad guys.

Charlie held up his hand. "You're one of my best deputies."

Leaving Samuel standing in the hallway grinning like a fool, he went into his office to put on his uniform.

A half hour later, during the drive out to Burt's double-wide at the edge of town, Charlie reviewed his plan of action with his deputy. Adrenaline was pumping through him, and he knew Samuel felt the same way. Charlie enjoyed everything about police work, especially getting out from behind his desk.

He wasn't normally a violent man, but when he

pictured poor Benito's bloody nose and split lip, and his fear, Charlie's grip on the steering wheel tightened. Obviously, the assault had been a smoke screen, intended to divert attention from Burt and his buddies.

"We'll keep this as simple as possible," he told Samuel as they pulled up in front of the mobile home. "But part of me almost hopes Burt decides not to cooperate."

Except for one wrong turn from the main highway, Robin didn't have much trouble finding the Bassett place, but it was full dark by the time she arrived. She drove slowly down the rutted dirt road, her headlights picking out heaps of junk and rusting farm machinery scattered along the fence line. A woman's figure appeared at the window of the old-fashioned farmhouse, but Robin was supposed to meet the rancher at the barn so she didn't stop.

Several mixed-breed dogs barked at her, and two of them ran around the car for a dozen yards before losing interest. Her car hit an especially deep pothole and bounced her hard against the seat, making her slow to a crawl. She'd be in a real pickle if she broke a spring.

At least the emergency call and the necessity of following Doc's directions had served one important purpose. They had kept her from thinking about Brian. On the flip side of the same coin, blocking out the flood of unwelcome memories had distracted her from worrying about this visit.

Or thinking about kissing Charlie.

Since the incident with Brian, not one man had tempted her to lower her guard—until now. Maybe the arrival of the alumni newsletter had been, if not a good thing, at least a reality check. A reminder to strengthen her resolve instead of opening herself up to heartache.

She didn't have any more time to speculate, because directly in front of her was the barn that Doc had described, and silhouetted in the open doorway was a short heavyset man who was obviously waiting for Robin. A cattle dog stood at his side.

When she pulled up and got out of her car, the dog bared its teeth and growled low in its throat. The action earned it a backhand slap to the head from its master.

"Shut up," he said.

Robin felt sorry for the poor mutt. It had only been doing its job.

"Mr. Bassett?" she asked as the man approached her car. "I'm Dr. Marlow. I believe Doc Harmon told you I'd be coming out."

He wasn't much taller than Robin, but he probably outweighed her by a hundred pounds. He was wearing a baseball cap, and his face was in shadow.

"You got any experience with bloat in cattle?" he asked gruffly, ignoring her attempt to introduce herself.

Robin chalked up his abruptness to concern for his livestock. Sometimes, for a variety of reasons, too much gas built up inside a cow. If the gas wasn't able to escape normally, it put too much pressure on the animal's heart and lungs. Without treatment, the problem could prove fatal.

"I've dealt with bloat before," she said as she pulled on her rubber boots. "Have you tubed the animal?"

"Naw. She was down when I found her, so I just stuck her with my pocket knife. All you need to do is sew her back up."

He'd eliminated the need for Robin to run a tube down the cow's throat, which was the usual treatment. If it was struggling to breathe, puncturing its side to release the gas was necessary in order to save its life. There wasn't much blood loss and the incision could be closed later, if the animal survived.

"If you'd show me where she is, I'll be happy to check her over," Robin said.

Bassett walked away, leaving her no choice but to grab her veterinary bag and clump along behind him into the barn. She had gotten used to the odor of healthy livestock, but the smell inside was rank, indicating filth and neglect. A sparse row of bare electric bulbs gave off a dull glow, illuminating several pairs of feline eyes in the shadows.

Bassett led her to a stall in which an Angus cow was confined.

"Do you have a better light?" Robin asked the rancher.

"Yeah, right here." He picked up a battery-powered lamp and switched it on so she could examine the bloody puncture.

It didn't take Robin long to clean and suture the wound. When she was done she peeled off her gloves and patted the cow's side. "Good girl," she murmured before she gathered up her equipment.

Bassett held the door of the stall open for her, and she gave him some brief follow-up instructions, even though she doubted he needed them. No doubt he had much more experience with cattle than Robin.

"You did a real nice job with that," he said, surprising her. She had tried to make conversation with him while she worked, but he'd been unresponsive.

"Thank you, Mr. Bassett." She completed the paperwork, a headache nagging at the edges of her consciousness. It had been a long day, and she'd be relieved to get home.

"Call me Paul," he said when she looked up. His face was coarse, with close-set eyes behind thick glasses and a scraggly beard threaded with gray. His sudden smile revealed stained teeth.

For the first time since Robin had arrived, she became aware of their isolation, surrounded by darkness in the deserted barn.

"Paul it is," she said briskly as she handed him her bill.

After he had studied it, his lips moving silently, he took out a worn leather wallet and paid her.

"I've got a bottle of scotch in the tack room," he said, moving closer. His little pig eyes stared at her without blinking, sending a shiver of discomfort sliding down her spine. "It's good stuff. Real smooth."

Robin tucked the money into her pocket nervously. He probably didn't even realize he was crowding her.

"Want to have a drink before you leave?" he asked.

She was at a loss how to respond, but she didn't want to offend a client, especially when she wasn't sure of local customs. It wasn't his fault that she found him physically repulsive.

Flustered, she glanced at her watch. "Oh, look at the time. I'd better not. I don't like to drink and drive." She was babbling now as she closed her bag. "I've got to be at work early, but thank you, anyway."

For a moment he didn't move. Something flashed across his face, something ugly. From somewhere outside, one of the dogs began barking. Paul glanced over his shoulder, and Robin gulped in a breath.

Turning back to her, he stepped away and held up his hands as if to ward her off. "Hey, hey, hey," he said. "I was just trying to be friendly, so don't go getting the wrong idea, okay?"

Had her discomfiture shown on her face? "No, oh, no. Of course not." She was backing away, holding her bag like a shield in front of her. Already she felt ridiculous. The poor man hadn't really done anything out of line.

She berated herself all the way to her car, continuing her one-sided discussion on the drive home. He hadn't said anything. So what if he had offered her a drink? It wasn't his fault she was over-sensitive. He probably offered Doc Harmon a drink when he was finished, too.

If she ever hoped to fit in around here, dealing with ranchers and tough Western types, she'd better loosen up. Otherwise she'd end up back in Chicago working at a "cats only" clinic with pink walls and fake flowers.

By the time Robin pulled into her driveway, she wasn't sure who to blame for the headache that was throbbing like the base on a car stereo.

All she knew for sure was that lowering her guard and kissing Charlie had been a really, really dumb idea.

Chapter Eight

"Are you going to the Waterloo Days picnic?"
Mae called over to Robin when she got out of her
VW the next evening. "It'll be at the city park to-
morrow after the parade."

Reluctantly Robin went over to the picket fence.
Had Mae seen Charlie bring her home the night before? Robin didn't feel like warding off nosy questions.

Since she'd first asked Mae not to collect her mail,
there hadn't been any more privacy problems. The
Simms were good landlords. Ed mowed Robin's lawn
when he did his own, and Mae frequently left cookies
or other goodies on her porch.

"I have to work in the clinic tomorrow," Robin
said after she'd walked over to the edge of her yard.

Mae was dressed in bright-yellow slacks and a matching plaid blouse. Her white hair looked as though it had been freshly styled.

"What a shame, dear," she exclaimed. "You'll miss all the fun. Will you be stuck at the clinic for the entire day?"

Robin didn't admit that she really didn't have to stay there as long as the answering service could reach her on her cell phone. "Doc's taking the weekend off," she said. "I guess he's going to be supervising the children's games at the picnic."

"Oh, that's right," Mae agreed. "He does that every year. The children really look forward to the way he includes them all."

All Robin knew about her boss's personal life was that he'd been widowed, but she resisted the chance to pump her chatty neighbor for information. If Doc wanted her to know anything, he'd tell her. She tried to respect his privacy, since Lord knew she had secrets of her own.

"I can't imagine a parade in a town as small as Waterloo," she said, waving to Ed as he came outside.

"Oh, we do a bang-up job of it," Mae replied. "It always starts with the mayor and his wife riding in a new convertible, followed by the school marching band and the cheer squad in the back of someone's pickup truck."

"Sounds exciting," Robin commented, suppressing a grin.

"Sure is," Ed drawled, shoving his hands deep into the pockets of his baggy pants. "We've got kids on bikes decorated with crepe paper streamers, rodeo riders on horseback and a couple of restored Chevies, if the owners get them waxed in time."

"Don't forget the lowriders," Mae added, clapping her hands together. "I love the way those cars go up and down."

"No floats?" Robin teased.

"One of the churches in Castle Rock usually sends something over," Ed replied, "and sometimes we get one from Denver." He elbowed Mae. "Did you remember to tell her about the quilt your sewing circle donated?"

"I almost forgot," she exclaimed. "We're selling raffle tickets to raise money for the women's shelter over in Kiowa. The winning number will be drawn at the picnic, but you don't have to be there for it."

It sounded like a worthwhile cause, so Robin took the hint. "How much are they?" she asked.

"A dollar each." Mae pulled a roll from her pocket. "Don't feel obligated, dear, but the quilt is beautiful, even if I do say so myself. The shelter's so deserving, and they have a support group, too."

Robin bought five tickets, and Ed wished her luck.

Mae leaned closer. "The town's just full of tourists, but the picnic's still a real family affair for the locals. You should try to come by."

"I'll keep it in mind," Robin replied, starting to back away.

"Have you talked to the sheriff today?" Mae asked, eyes twinkling behind her thick lenses. "I suppose he's running himself ragged with all the tourists in town. A few people always celebrate a little too much, you know."

"I suppose that's true." Robin decided to call Mae's bluff. "Why did you ask if I'd talked to him?"

"I thought you might have heard. Vonnie Roderick called me." Mae glanced around, as though she was looking for potential eavesdroppers. "Vonnie heard from her daughter who's dating the dispatcher that last night they arrested the gang who's responsible for all the burglaries!"

Ed hitched up his trousers. "It wasn't actually a gang, honey. Parker down at the barber shop told me they hauled in three guys."

"Was anyone hurt?" Robin hadn't really given much thought to the potential danger in being sheriff even in a town as small as Waterloo.

Ed shook his head. "Parker would have mentioned if they were. All he said was that three guys are in the pokey."

"That's good to know," Robin said. "Have a nice day tomorrow."

"Try to come by the park," Mae said. "And good luck with the raffle."

With a parting wave, Robin went into her house. Between Waterloo Days and Charlie's Heart, he'd be too busy to give her a thought. There was a softball game tomorrow and a rodeo that ran through Sunday.

She told herself she was relieved. She needed time to think. Erline had invited her to go to the club again tonight, but Robin wasn't ready to face Charlie. Not until she got her attraction to him back under control.

She looked in the refrigerator, but nothing appeared remotely appetizing and she was out of frozen dinners. The grocery store was on the main street, which had been closed off for a street fair and swap meet tonight. Emma's Café would be mobbed and so would the drive-in.

She didn't feel like dealing with crowds, so she rooted around in the cupboard until she found some crackers. Too bad she'd stuck the empty peanut butter jar back on the shelf. The package of cheese in the fridge had gone moldy and the bottle of soda was flat, so she washed down the crackers with a glass of water.

She was too restless to watch television and there was nothing to read, so she decided to work off some of her excess energy by cleaning the bathroom. She pulled on a faded, oversize T-shirt that had been left behind by an old roommate. ''Neil Diamond Summer Tour'' was written across the front and it was nearly long enough to cover her purple sweatpants. They were spattered with paint, and she'd hacked off the legs.

Since the bathroom was still warm, she opened the window. Aerosmith was cranked up on the CD player, but the yards were big and it wasn't late. Her bangs were already sticking to her forehead, so she dug a neon-orange sweatband from the back of her drawer and pulled it on, fluffing her hair absently with her fingers.

She was nearly finished wiping out the bathtub and Cher's latest hit had replaced Aerosmith when Robin heard hammering above the driving beat of the music. One of the neighbors must be building something in his garage.

Robin stood back to admire her cleaning job, grinding her hips back and forth as she belted out the final chorus along with Cher. Something moved in Robin's peripheral vision and the last notes froze in her throat.

She stared at Charlie's face through the open window. He was grinning as he looked back at her.

Cher ended the number without Robin's help, followed by a moment of dead silence.

"Hi." Politely Charlie tugged on the brim of his Stetson. "Nice job on the song."

Robin hit the off button on the CD player. "Uh, thanks." Water from the wet sponge she was squeezing dripped onto her bare feet. "What are you doing here?"

"I've been pounding on your side door for ten minutes," he replied. "I got concerned that the pizza I brought over would get stone cold before you heard me."

"Pizza?" she echoed. Her stomach growled a protest of the meager snack she'd fed it earlier.

"Half pepperoni and sausage, half vegetarian," he said with a glance down at her noisy midsection. "I wasn't sure what you liked, but it sounds like I got here just in time.''

''Just in time for what?'' It seemed that all she could do was parrot what he was saying. ''I thought you'd either be on duty all evening or running your place.''

''Even officers of the law get an occasional dinner break,'' he drawled. ''Want to let me in, or are you too busy scrubbing toilets to eat?'' His gaze left her face, his smirk reminding Robin of how she must look in her bizarre housecleaning costume.

''Only one toilet,'' she replied, ''but technically I was still wiping out the tub.'' Why was she bothering to explain? Did she actually think she could salvage her dignity?

He lifted his gaze to her neon-orange sweatband. ''Ah, my mistake.''

Hastily she tossed the sponge into the sink and yanked the offending band off her head. She probably resembled an acid rocker on a bad day, but she refused to glance in the mirror. Instead she peeled off one rubber glove and ran her fingers through her hair.

''Why don't you come around to the door?'' she suggested, hiding her annoyance that he'd caught her dressed like a thrift store reject and singing off-key. ''Unless, of course, you'd rather crawl through the window.''

For a moment he seemed to consider it. ''Guess not,'' he said. ''It's a big tourist weekend, and I might ruin the crease in my uniform slacks.''

"Whatever," Robin muttered under her breath.

When she met him at the door, he was holding the pizza box in one hand and a six-pack of root beer in the other.

"Didn't sound like you'd already eaten." He walked past her into the kitchen and set down the pizza.

So he hadn't missed her stomach's growling response to his announcement that he had come bearing food.

"I wasn't hungry when I got home," she said defensively, arms folded across her chest in the futile hope of hiding the Neil Diamond logo.

Charlie ignored her hostile tone. "How about now? Want some pizza?"

Defeated, she waved a hand at the table. "Have a seat, unless you're worried it will ruin your crease."

"Do I look worried?" Turning a chair around, he straddled it and rested his arms on the back.

Robin opened the cupboard. She took out two plates and plunked them down. "Do you want ice for your soda?"

Charlie had been trying to read her mood, to figure out whether she was glad to see him or not. When he'd first seen her through the bathroom window, he had wanted to lean in and kiss her, but the sill was too high. Besides, he'd remembered how startled she'd been when he'd tried it before, when they'd been riding.

Now her body language, as she bustled around her

kitchen, screamed, ''Don't touch.'' She might as well be wearing a shirt with a No Trespassing sign on the front.

Perhaps she just didn't like pepperoni. Or maybe she didn't like *him*.

His luck had been bound to run out sooner or later, but why now? And why with this woman?

''Ice would be great,'' he replied, digging into his shirt pocket. ''I brought straws.'' He held them out in an attempt to be helpful.

She stuck them into two mismatched glasses. ''Mae told me you arrested someone for the burglaries,'' she said.

Charlie popped the tops on two cans of root beer. ''Yeah, we did. Have you heard who?''

She shook her head. ''I haven't met a lot of low-lifes since I moved here, unless you count a couple of questionable guys at your place.''

''I'll have to tell the bouncer to be more selective,'' he deadpanned. ''Well, you didn't meet the alleged burglars at Charlie's Heart, but you and I were together when you saw them.''

Her gaze clouded with confusion. ''Oh?''

He waited silently as he watched her mind work. ''No way!''

''Way,'' he contradicted with a laugh. ''It was the same trio you and I tangled with behind the auction barn.''

Her eyes widened. ''That doesn't make any sense. They accused your waiter. That's why they were has-

sling him, wasn't it?'' She leaned against the counter.
''Are you sure they're guilty?''

''Actually, Benito is a dishwasher, not a waiter.
And Burt, the guy who hit him, has denied everything. Unfortunately for Burt, one of his buddies
rolled over.'' Charlie winked. ''It was the skilled police work that tripped him up.'' He lowered his voice
secretively and told her what Samuel had found out.

''It's good to know you caught them,'' she said.
''I'm sure a lot of people are resting easier.''

Charlie was busy checking out the length of her
bare legs below the ragged edges of her shorts. ''I've
only got a half hour before I have to get back,'' he
said regretfully, ''and even that's just if I don't get a
call. Everyone is spelling each other so we can all
eat, but when the bars close, I'll need every badge
I've got available.'' The night before, they'd had several fights, a pickpocketing complaint, a child lost for
a few minutes at the carnival before his parents found
him, and a minor car accident.

Robin joined Charlie at the table, disappointing him
by not appearing crushed that he couldn't stay longer.
''It was nice of you to bring this by,'' she said instead
as she put a piece of vegetarian pizza on her plate.

He'd have to settle for that. For now. ''I owed
you.'' Famished, he bit into a slice covered with pepperoni and sausage.

She sipped on her soda, looking puzzled. ''Did we
have a bet about something?''

Charlie had been thinking how sexy she looked in

the oversize T-shirt that made a man want to skim his hands under the hem and explore the shape hidden by its loose folds. Damn, but he had it bad, he thought, as he chewed and swallowed.

"I promised you pizza last night," he reminded her. She hadn't even remembered! "I didn't want you to think I don't deliver on my promises."

Robin merely lifted her brows, ignoring his comment.

Just this afternoon a blonde with a great body packed into a skimpy top and the shortest cutoffs he'd ever seen had come on to him like a coyote attacking a rabbit. She'd explained in a husky slice-of-Texas accent that she was a barrel racer in town for the rodeo.

And looking for a little fun on the side, she'd added as her gaze slid over him with the subtlety of a blow-torch. Her sly smile had filled in the rest of her intentions.

Uncomplicated sex. No expectations, no inhibitions and no regrets.

She'd taken a deep breath, straining the fabric of her halter top, and Charlie's eyes had nearly crossed. He'd never been big on one-night stands, but she wasn't leaving until Sunday. A two-night stand if a fellow had a streak of luck…and a pack of stamina.

So what had Charlie done, faced with that kind of offer? Made a date for later? Given her his cell number? Taken the room key she'd dangled in front of him like bait?

Oh, hell, no. Not straight-arrow Charlie, who hadn't been laid for longer than he cared to remember.

When a lie about two kids and a pregnant wife waiting at home hadn't cooled the blonde's interest, he'd tossed in a broken rib and a trick knee.

The trick knee seemed to intrigue her, but he'd stood firm.

A short time later he'd seen her leave arm in arm with one of the busboys. Charlie hadn't felt a twinge of regret. All he'd been able to think about was finding enough time to come by Robin's. What was wrong with him?

Now she was treating him with all the warmth she would give the Pizza Palace delivery man.

Charlie considered telling her about the blonde, but sanity prevailed. He'd learned back in junior high that girls didn't handle comparisons very well.

"Is everything okay?" he asked instead.

Robin had been poking at the olives on her pizza. She lifted her head and eyed him warily. "What do you mean?"

He shrugged. "Tough day?"

She nibbled on a mushroom slice while she considered her reply. "No, I guess not," she said finally. "Nothing unusual."

He was tempted to ask if she'd given him a thought since their kiss, but he hated to come across as pathetic. "What's new?" he asked. "Any aches and pains from riding Pansy?"

"Actually not. And I even got called out last night," she replied, and then she bit her lip as if she regretted mentioning anything.

"Didn't it go well?" He helped himself to another piece of pizza, even though he didn't really want it. He knew he was in for a long night, one of the busiest of the year, and he had to eat. There'd be no time for refueling later.

"What do you mean?" Now she sounded a little defensive. Did she think he was questioning her ability as a vet?

"I don't know." He waved one hand, not used to explaining everything he said. "Did the animal die?"

She shook her head. "Oh. Oh, no. It was a pretty little Angus heifer with bloat. The owner had already stuck her with his pocket knife, so all I had to do was sew her up."

Charlie knew all about bloat in cattle. "I was a rancher in my previous life," he reminded her. "I've tubed a few head."

"Amateur stuff," Robin said. "Have you ever had to stick one?"

He nodded. "I remember once when there wasn't time to run the tube down the heifer's throat, so Dad punched a hole in her rumen. I thought the gas being released was pretty hilarious, so the next time he handed me the trocar and made me jab her myself. I threw up afterward, but I learned my lesson."

"How old were you?" Robin asked.

He remembered to this day how scared he'd been

that he would kill the poor miserable heifer. "Ten, I think. Maybe twelve."

"Good gravy," she exclaimed. "What lesson could you possibly have learned at that age?"

He frowned. "That suffering is never funny." And not to get caught laughing by the old man, he added silently.

Before Robin could say anything else, Charlie's cell phone rang. He glanced down at the number.

"I have to take this," he explained. "It's Adam."

Robin watched Charlie's changing expressions while he listened to his brother. She wondered how his nose had gotten broken. Maybe she'd ask him sometime.

While she was sneaking cautious glances at him, not wishing to be caught staring, he took a small notebook from his pocket and leafed through the pages.

"I'm sorry, bro," he said. "That didn't pan out. I traced Mickey Barstow over to Wyoming, and the rancher I talked to said Mickey's been working for him for six weeks."

Robin watched the way Charlie's mouth shaped the words as he talked. The name he'd mentioned must have been a suspect he'd investigated. It sounded as though his brothers' spread had been hit again.

"No, not this weekend, but I'll be out the first of the week." He listened, his grim expression finally softening. "Sure thing. How long will you be around? Yeah, I'll try to come by." He caught Robin staring and he winked at her as he ended the call.

"Now I've really got to go," he told her as he slid back his chair. "Duty calls."

"Is everything all right?" she asked as he got to his feet. "It sounded like your brother got hit again. Any leads?"

Charlie shook his head. "Checked out a couple of former employees who've left the area. Both had alibis. We're still looking at a couple of other things." He touched her arm. "Maybe I'll run into you. Going to the picnic tomorrow?"

She hesitated, fighting conflicting feelings of attraction and wariness. "I'm not sure. I'll be at the clinic for most of the day."

"Maybe I'll stop by if I get a chance. Meanwhile, Adam said to be sure to look for his bunch, if you do go. There will be plenty of food, and Rory makes the best fried chicken in Elbert County." He glanced over his shoulder. "Just don't let what I said slip in front of Adam's wife."

"That was sweet of him to include me." Robin's hands were clasped together. "And it was nice of you to bring the pizza. Thank you."

Charlie moved closer. "He's sweet, but I'm only nice?" he teased. "Why is that?"

She couldn't think of a reply, so she merely shrugged.

Charlie's smile faded as his dark eyes searched her face. "Sure you're okay?" he persisted.

"Except for having to finish cleaning the bathroom."

He leaned closer, hesitated. Gaze locked on hers. He must not have seen what he was looking for, because he straightened and sighed.

"Okay," he said. "Later." He turned to go, his shoulders looking impossibly wide in the tan shirt.

"Charlie." His name escaped before she could press her lips together and prevent it from slipping out.

He spun back around as though he'd been waiting for her to speak. "What?"

Helpless to stop herself, she reached for him.

He scooped her into his arms, pulling her close as he bent his head to meet her halfway. His mouth covered hers in a fevered kiss. Hungry for more of him, she opened for his questing tongue and buried her fingers in the hair at his nape. Her breasts were flattened against the hard muscles of his chest, and his embrace was like a vise as he held her.

His tongue dipped and stroked. His lips nibbled. A delicious shiver went through her, even though she felt far from cold, and she crowded closer still.

He groaned, changing the angle of the kiss. She cupped his face in her hands and traced the shape of his upper lip with the tip of her tongue. He dove again, caressing, tasting, his passion making her head spin and her blood race.

Her body was boneless as she melted against him, her body as pliant as hot candle wax. He slipped his fingers beneath the loose hem of her sleeve to caress the sensitive skin there and then he wrapped his hands around her upper arms. He nibbled his way along her jawline and drew the lobe of her ear between his lips. Reaction shot through her and he made a harsh sound, deep in his throat. Gently he tightened his grip on her arms as he straightened away from her.

"Damn," he said with obvious regret. "I wish I could stay. I should have left fifteen minutes ago." He let her go carefully. "I could come back, but it's going to be a late night. I might have to wake you." As he looked down at her, with his face flushed and a question in his dark eyes, Robin realized what he was asking.

"I'm sorry," she said, feeling like a naive fool as she backed away. "I have to be at the clinic first thing." She crossed her arms over her chest. It was her own fault he'd gotten the wrong idea. Instead of letting him leave, she'd thrown herself at him.

He cleared his throat. "Hey," he said softly, "I didn't mean to make you feel pressured. You really get to me, babe, and I lost my head for a second."

Robin looked up at him, relieved that he didn't appear angry with her hot-and-cold dance.

She nodded, wrapping her arms tighter around her middle. He confused her, and her feelings confused her even more. "Okay."

He frowned and glanced at the door. "I have to go or Samuel will kill me. He's the one I'm supposed to relieve. You and I will talk later. About this, about…whatever we need to. Okay?"

Again she bobbed her head, trying to figure him

out. "Go ahead." She trailed after him to the door. "I didn't mean to make you late getting back."

Humor lit his eyes. "I'm the boss," he reminded her as he pressed his finger to her lips. "Don't say you didn't mean it."

"Be careful," she called after him as she remembered the danger that could be lurking out there whenever he put on a star and a gun.

He stuck up his hand in response, but he didn't turn back to look at her until he was getting into his Jeep. Before he backed out of the driveway, he blew her a kiss.

She hoped Mae and Ed were still at the potluck down at the Grange Hall.

It was early afternoon when hunger finally drove Robin out of the clinic. She'd been updating files, answering the phone, and she'd treated two patients.

One was a black Lab with ear mites and the other a horse with an abrasion on its foreleg. The gorgeous palomino was in town for the parade and the rodeo. His owner had noticed the scrape after the parade, so he'd trailered his horse straight to the clinic. The fancy red and gold paint job matched his truck.

After she'd spread ointment on the wound and bandaged it, Robin advised him to skip the calf roping competition the next day, and he'd agreed.

Even Erline had come by earlier to pick up a crocheted wrap she'd forgotten and introduced Robin to the man she had in tow. The two of them had been on their way over to Charlie's for lunch.

Wyatt was skinny as a fence post, with thinning hair and a prominent Adam's apple, but the admiration on his face when he looked at the clinic receptionist made Robin happy for Erline and sorry for herself.

Charlie had driven by twice, that she noticed, in his Cherokee with its official star on the side and the rack of lights on top, but he hadn't stopped. Who could blame him after last night? Her hot-and-cold attitude had probably given him frostbite, hard to come by in Colorado at the end of July.

Now she switched the phones over to the answering service, flipped over the Open sign and locked the front door of the clinic. She was intent on a deli sandwich or a burger at the drive-in. She was about to get into the Rabbit, when Adam Winchester's black pickup pulled up beside her.

He poked his head out the window. "Coming to the picnic?" he asked. He was wearing a baseball cap and a blue plaid shirt with the sleeves rolled up.

"I thought I'd just grab a sandwich," she replied.

It was the first time she'd seen Adam without his black Resistol. He'd corrected her gently when she'd called it a Stetson. Now he looked more like a neighbor than the head of a ranching empire. His grin was bracketed by grooves that were etched into his weathered skin, and the hair beneath his cap was going silver.

"Come on," he said, leaning over to open the passenger door. "Get in."

Rory lifted her eyebrows. "Where are we going?"

"I'm taking you to the picnic," he said. "The women have been cooking for three days, and we've got more food than we could ever eat."

Robin hesitated. If Charlie was there, would he think she was following him?

"Got a cell phone?" Adam asked.

She nodded, patting her bag. "Right here."

"I'll run you back here when you're ready," he said. "My daughter's visiting from Seattle and I'd like you to meet her."

Robin was curious about the girl. She'd thought David was his son, and the family dynamics were still mostly a mystery. If she did see Charlie, she could always blame Adam for abducting her.

"What's your daughter's name?" she asked.

"Kim." His smile went crooked, and he managed to inject the short word with a wealth of affection and regret. "She's twenty."

Robin climbed in beside Adam, intrigued by the glimpse of human frailty he'd shown. "You must be happy to have her home."

His grin faded as he backed out of the parking lot. "Seattle's been her home for the past five years. I don't see her nearly as much as I'd like." He glanced at Robin with hooded eyes, as though aware he'd revealed more than he wanted. "You're right, though. It's nice to have her back." A muscle flexed along his jaw. "It's just hard to say goodbye every time she leaves."

Robin didn't know what to say in reply to his frankness, so she remained silent.

As they turned off the main street, she saw the people wandering up and down the old-fashioned sidewalk that ran in front of the skinny, false-fronted buildings. The street fair had drawn quite a crowd. A Ferris wheel, part of the carnival that had been set up in the sale barn parking lot, loomed above the downtown buildings.

"Is it always this crowded during the festival?" Robin asked Adam as he slowed behind a minibus disgorging passengers.

"Pretty much," he replied. "We get people from Denver and all the surrounding towns, as well as the locals who come in. It's great for all the businesses, and Charlie said his club's been packed every night this week." The bus started up again, and Adam followed it. "Of course, that's more from Rory's singing than all these tourists. Have you heard her yet?"

"Oh, yes. She's got a great voice. So does Charlie."

"He's got an ear for music," Adam replied. "He pretty much taught himself piano and guitar."

He slammed on the brakes as an older couple stepped into the street in front of his truck without bothering to look first.

"Bless them all," he muttered. "This was a mistake. I should have gone the other way."

It was too late now. There was more traffic behind them and pedestrians all over the place. "I thought everyone would be at the picnic," Robin said.

"Don't I wish," he replied as they finally got through the worst part. "It's more a chance to socialize with the neighbors we haven't seen since the Christmas pageant over at the school."

His description of small-town life made Robin hunger for something she hadn't felt since her aunt's passing—to really put down roots and make a home for herself.

"There's no parking anywhere close," Adam told her as he drove down the street edging the park. "There's David and his girlfriend. I'll drop you off."

He tooted the horn to get their attention as he pulled up to the curb.

"Thanks for fetching me," Robin said, hoping Adam would understand that she was grateful for more than just that.

He reached over to pat her hand. "You're a part of the community now. Might as well get used to it."

Chapter Nine

After David introduced Robin to his girlfriend, Joey, the three of them made their way through the human maze that covered the park lawn. Robin's nervousness faded as people waved and called out friendly greetings. It didn't seem to matter if they'd met her or not.

Groups of children ran shrieking between picnic tables where adults sat and visited. Blankets were spread on the grass. Lawn chairs and coolers were clustered in the shade of the stately old trees. Food was everywhere.

The music changed with each group they passed, from rock to country to classical. The sounds reminded Robin of a patchwork quilt, each square different, but all of them framed by a border of shared laughter.

"There's the Winchester brood." David pointed to a picnic table covered with dishes and surrounded by people. Some were seated on the benches and folding chairs. Others were standing. Rory's bright-red hair was a beacon as she and Travis talked to a dark-haired girl, but Robin didn't see Charlie.

Disappointment tangled with relief.

On the grass near the table were several plastic ice chests and tote bags. Toys and a frisbee were scattered on a blanket, and a baby dozed in an infant seat, guarded by a gray-haired woman in a reclining lawn chair.

As David motioned Robin forward the conversation around the table died and her nervousness returned.

"Hey, it's the new vet," Travis called out. "Hi, Robin." He glanced at David. "You doing the honors?"

"I'll try," David replied as Joey slipped her arm through his and leaned closer. "This is Robin Marlowe. She won't remember all your names, so give her a break, okay? I've been in the family for five years, and I still can't keep all the kids straight."

"That's because we keep having more," Travis drawled.

Rory groaned. A couple of people laughed, and the rest smiled at Robin.

David began pointing and rattling off names. "That's Rory with the orange hair."

"Auburn!" she corrected him.

"No way, Red!" Travis exclaimed.

More laughter. Rory batted his arm.

David plowed on. "My gorgeous mother, Emily, who's married to Adam."

"Thank you, son," said a pretty blonde.

"Our friend, Rita."

Robin recognized the waitress from Charlie's.

"This is Betty, who was Adam's housekeeper until she retired."

"Until the lot of you wore me out," the gray-haired woman corrected him. She lifted her hand in greeting to Robin. "Do you treat cats?" she asked. "I've got six."

"Yes, of course," she replied. "Group rates for more than a half dozen."

"Betty, is that your youngest?" David asked, pointing to the sleeping infant.

Her cheeks turned pink. "Behave yourself. I'm watching him for Amy Whitecastle."

"Oh, I almost forgot," David said. "Last but not least, of course. That's Kim, Adam's daughter."

The girl who'd been talking to Rory and Travis tossed back her long, dark hair and smiled. "Hi, Robin."

"Come and sit by me," Adam's wife invited, patting the bench next to her.

"She won't bite," David said in a stage whisper. "No teeth."

"Ha-ha," she replied. "David, dearest, would you round up the kids. We're going to eat as soon as Adam gets back."

"He was looking for a parking space," Robin said as she sat down, grateful for the friendly overture. "He may be a while." She would have liked to ask about Charlie, but Travis saved her the trouble.

"Has anyone seen the sheriff?" he asked.

His query was met with shrugs and shaking heads, just as Adam walked up.

"Charlie's working the crowd," he replied. "He said to save him a chicken leg." Adam bent over his wife. As their lips met and lingered, a young boy who'd run up to stand between Travis and Rory let out a catcall.

Adam broke off the kiss and pointed a threatening finger at the boy. "Steven," he exclaimed, trying hard to glower and failing. "How old are you?"

The boy looked surprised. "I'm ten, Uncle Adam."

"Want to see eleven?"

Steven stuck out his tongue and then ducked behind his dad.

David and Joey returned, holding hands, followed by a pack of noisy children. For the next few minutes there was bedlam as Emily and Rory uncovered and arranged dishes and platters of food, Betty supervised the washing of faces and hands, Kim picked up the baby, who had begun to fuss, and Travis surprised Robin by setting out plastic utensils and paper plates.

Organization rose from apparent chaos. After everyone had helped themselves, Robin found herself sitting in a lawn chair with a plate of food and a glass of lemonade. Conversation ebbed and flowed as everyone ate. When they were done, the children asked politely to be excused.

Charlie arrived as they were leaving. Amid the chorus of greetings, he leaned down to Robin. "You okay?" he mouthed.

She returned his smile and patted her stomach. "Full as a tick." Contentment washed over her.

He lifted his gaze. "Did the locusts leave anything for me?" he demanded. "I'm starving."

"Sit down, and I'll fix you a plate," Rory replied.

As she started to rise, Travis laid his hand on her shoulder. "Take it easy, babe. I'll feed the brat."

She covered his hand with hers. "See why I love this guy?" she asked no one in particular.

"That's Sheriff Brat to you, bro," Charlie called out.

After he'd given Kim a hug, chucked the baby's chin and kissed Betty's cheek, he pulled up a folding chair next to Robin. "Did you meet everyone?"

"Yes," she replied. "You've got a wonderful family."

"I'll have to agree with that," Travis replied as he handed Charlie a plate heaped with chicken and salads. "You want a root beer? There's some in the cooler."

"Thanks. That's as close to a real brewski as I'll get this weekend."

After Travis had handed him a cold soda, Charlie began eating. "Sorry about that," he told Robin after a couple of mouthfuls. "I haven't had a bite of food since six this morning."

"That's okay. You were right about the chicken." While he ate, she watched everyone around her and listened to bits of conversations.

At one point she tipped her head and looked up at the sky through narrowed eyes. The brilliant blue was filtered through the branches of a tall cottonwood, one of many mature trees scattered throughout the park.

Despite the noise and the people—and the fact that the best-looking man in town was sitting beside her—she felt relaxed.

When Robin opened her eyes she found Charlie studying her intently. She sat up straighter and blinked a couple of times.

"Oh, my God," she exclaimed. "How long was I asleep?" She looked around, but no one else was paying them the slightest attention. David and his girlfriend were lying on a quilt over by an oak tree while Kim sat on the picnic bench, deep in conversation with two other girls her age. Every once in a while, she tossed her long hair and glanced over at—if Robin understood the dynamics of the family tree—her stepbrother. He, on the other hand, appeared to be totally engrossed with his pretty blond girlfriend.

"Asleep?" Charlie echoed after he'd drained the soda can. "And here I thought you were merely resting your eyes from my dazzling presence." He crumpled the can in one hand. "I'm crushed."

"Whatever. How long was I out?" Robin asked

again, unable to withstand his grin. She rolled her eyes. The man was truly incorrigible.

"You were asleep for less than five minutes, about as long as it took me to clean my plate." He glanced longingly at the food still on the table, and then he got to his feet. "Be right back."

Someone had covered the bowls and put all the trash into a plastic bag.

"I can't believe there are brownies left!" he exclaimed, holding up a plate covered with plastic wrap. "Want one?"

Robin considered turning down chocolate for about a nanosecond. "Yes, please."

He brought two of them on napkins and handed one to her.

"So, what do you think of my relatives, now that you've met them all?" he asked. "Want to marry me? I'll throw in a free membership to the family and passes to all Winchester events."

Robin was too busy trying not to choke on her brownie to reply.

"Marry you?" she finally sputtered when she could breathe again. "Are you insane?"

He laid his hand over his heart. "You wound me, woman. It was a serious offer."

"One I'd be careful of tossing around or some woman is going to accept, as ridiculous as that may seem." She shook her finger at him. "Then where will you be, smarty-pants?"

"Married, I guess." He shrugged. "My brothers seem to be happy."

Robin felt an uncomfortable twinge at the idea of Charlie married to someone else.

"So what did you think of the brood?" he asked again.

Grateful for the change of subject, she told him that she'd enjoyed meeting them all and how welcome they'd made her feel.

"We all seem to get along okay," he said. "No major personality clashes, which is kind of nice."

Robin leaned closer and lowered her voice, even though no one was near enough to overhear. "What's with David and Adam's daughter, Kim?" she asked. "Their parents are married to each other, but I haven't seen the two of them exchange three words."

Charlie's brows rose, and he glanced in their direction. "That's odd. They were good friends before she moved to Seattle with her mom. Maybe a little too good." He scratched his jaw absently. "Did Kim show you her ring? She just got engaged to some guy back in Seattle, and I don't think Adam's too pleased about it."

"I haven't seen it yet," Robin replied. "We didn't really get a chance to talk. Does he think she's too young?"

"It's partly that. She's only twenty. Adam and Kim's mother got married while they were in college, and it didn't work out. But I think the main reason is Adam's been hoping she'd eventually come back to stay. Her fiancé's family all live in Seattle, so her moving back is probably not going to happen.''

Robin remembered Adam's expression when he'd told her about Kim. ''I could tell that he misses her,'' she said. ''How old was Kim when her parents divorced?''

''She was only a baby,'' Charlie replied, his gaze on his niece. In snug white jeans and a tiny coral top that drew attention to her slim figure and dark-brown hair, she was a beautiful young woman. ''Adam raised her, with Betty's help, until Kim was fifteen.''

''Isn't that unusual?'' Robin was shamelessly curious about the members of Charlie's family.

He propped one boot on the other knee and rested his hand on it. ''Our old man dropped dead while Adam was in college, so he had to come home and take over or we would have lost the ranch. At about that same time, Christie found out she was pregnant. Adam did the right thing, and they tried to make a go of it, but she was a city girl and the winters on a ranch can be harsh.'' He glanced down at his hand, resting on his boot. ''It's probably even worse when a woman's expecting. I don't remember a lot about it. I was still in high school, and we were all working like dogs to keep things going. He built that house for her, where he lives now, but he came home one day and she was gone.''

''Kim?'' Robin asked.

''No, Adam's wife. She'd left Kim with one of the wrangler's wives and never looked back. Fifteen years later, she contacted Kim. The next thing we all knew, the two of them had moved to Seattle.'' He sighed. ''When Kim left, I think Emily was the one who kept him going.''

''Did he and Kim get along?'' Robin was still struggling to understand how a mother could walk out on her baby and not keep in touch.

Charlie seemed to hesitate, as though he was picking his words. ''Adam was different from the way he is now,'' he said finally. ''He was pretty strict with her. He and Emily had their hands full, trying to keep David away from Kim while they were busy falling for each other.''

''David and Kim seem to have gotten over that now,'' Robin exclaimed dryly. Adam's stepson stood up and scooped Joey into his arms. They both shrieked with laughter as he spun her in a circle. After one quick glance, Kim had turned with her back to the other two. She said something to her friends, and the three of them hooted with laughter of their own.

''I wonder what's really going on,'' Charlie murmured, half to himself. ''David doesn't usually act like such a show-off. He's pretty levelheaded, and I didn't think he and Joey were that close.''

''They all seem so darned young,'' Robin grumbled.

Charlie got to his feet and held out his hand. ''Come on, Methuselah. Duty calls. I'll drop you off at the clinic. Is your car over there?''

"Yes, but Adam said he'd take me back. I don't want him to wonder where I went."

Charlie hadn't let go of her hand. "Don't worry about it. I already told him I'd deal with you myself."

When they got to the clinic, Charlie insisted on following Robin inside after she'd unlocked the front door.

"With the rodeo and the carnival in town, there are a lot of creeps around," he said as he glanced into the tiny examining rooms. "You can't be too careful."

Although he believed in the wisdom of what he was saying, part of him felt like a fraud. It wasn't strangers Robin should be concerned about, it was him. He was so hungry for her he could have taken her on the surgery table, if she'd been willing.

"Thank you," she said, her hands clasped together in front of her. "No one's paged me. I'm going to check for messages and then I think I'll go on home." Her gaze lingered on his for half a heartbeat longer than necessary. When she finally glanced away, her eyelids fluttered and she was blushing.

He wondered how much experience she'd actually had with men. The way she jumped back and forth between returning his kisses with a passion that scorched him right down to the soles of his feet and a hesitation that was almost awkward, it was as though she couldn't tell that he was interested.

Make that mesmerized.

He'd never been a man who worried about rejection. Usually he just dove right in. If the woman didn't feel the same way, they ended up friends.

Coming to a decision, he glanced at the big front windows, blinds open to the street, and grabbed her by the wrist.

"Come with me, okay?" He led her to the room in the back.

She resisted for a moment, her eyes wide, but then she let him lead her.

Just to be on the safe side, in case anyone came in, he shut the door behind them. Lucky for him, the pens and cages were all empty. He didn't need an audience, even a four-legged one, for what he was about to do.

"What's going on?" she asked with a worried glance at the door.

Charlie let go of her wrist and gripped her shoulders in both hands. He had a gift for ad-libbing, but he didn't want to mess this up.

He stared into her face, still trying to figure out what it was about her that had hooked him like a fish. She was pretty, but it wasn't just her looks. She had more courage than she realized, more spirit. And she kissed like an angel.

"Charlie?" Her voice quavered. She probably thought he'd lost his mind.

"I wanted you to know that I think you're a very special woman," he began, intending to feel his way as he went. To his utter shock, her eyes filled with tears and she pulled away.

"That's not quite the reaction I was aiming for," he said.

She looked up, her eyelids fluttering as though she was trying to blink away the tears. "Are you dumping me?" she asked in a tiny voice. "Not that we had anything serious going, and I understand, I really do. You just caught me off guard, that's all."

"Dumping you!" he echoed, incredulous. So much for his talent for improvisation! "I'm nuts about you!" If she didn't return his interest, would she be crying? Taking her tears as a positive sign, he wrapped his arms around her and lowered his head.

Charlie poured every bit of what he was feeling into the kiss he gave her. He was vaguely aware that she was hanging on to him as tightly as he held her. When they finally had no choice but to break for air or die of suffocation, he lifted his head.

"Tell me I'm not alone in this," he pleaded. His entire body felt as though it was on fire. If he'd been a demolition expert instead of a cop, he would have blown them both up.

Robin's lips trembled, and fresh tears filled her eyes.

"So now you're dumping me," he joked, but he had to swallow the sudden lump in his throat. What if he'd misread her? What if she didn't find him attractive? Maybe it was just the uniform.

She lifted a hand that trembled, and laid it along his cheek.

"I like you, too," she said.

Charlie squeezed his eyes shut as relief coursed through him. The simple declaration was the sweetest he had ever heard.

Before he could say anything else, a cell phone started ringing.

"Damn," he exclaimed. "I knew I was pushing it."

"It's my phone that's ringing, not yours," Robin said, glancing down. "The answering service wouldn't call if it wasn't important. I'm sorry, but I need to take it."

"Aren't we a pair?" Charlie said, leaning down to give her a quick, hard kiss. "Could I take you to dinner on Monday? That's the first time off I'll have."

"I'd like that." Her smile seemed more genuine than any she'd given him so far. Maybe they'd moved on to the next level of their relationship, although with Robin he wasn't even sure what the next level was.

They said a quick goodbye, and she took her phone call while he let himself out, wondering if anyone would notice that their gun-toting sheriff had more on his mind than chasing bad guys. Anyone armed with a dangerous weapon should make sure his blood supply stayed above his belt, preferably somewhere in the vicinity of his brain, or he was liable to do something stupid, like shooting off his own toe.

Charlie allowed himself one smirk as he hitched up his belt and relegated Robin to the part of his mind marked Monday. He was an adult, not a horny kid, he reminded himself, and he could do this. Or take cold showers until Monday evening.

"Tell me all the bits and pieces of your life that I don't know," Charlie suggested from across the linen-covered expanse that separated them.

She twirled her wineglass and studied him in the seductive lighting of the Italian restaurant. An attentive waiter stayed just this side of hovering while a strolling violinist played discreetly.

When Charlie had called her at work, he'd refused to say where he was taking her, just that it was nice and he thought she'd enjoy it. So here she was in a restaurant that had once been a Victorian home built by pioneers, in a town called Sedalia. She was wearing the same dress she'd had on when she'd danced with him. Charlie was breathtaking in a Western-cut charcoal-gray suit that hugged his broad shoulders, over a paler-gray shirt with a black string tie. For once his head was bare. If this dating thing was going to become a habit, she'd have to run up to Denver and buy some new clothes.

Meanwhile, she found herself telling him quite a few of those bits he'd asked about. They discussed schooling and family, hobbies, music and goals.

She wanted her own practice someday, while he was torn between a career in law enforcement and running his club.

"Being sheriff is more politics than cop work," he said. "It's keeping too many people happy, and I'm not sure I'm the right man for it. Besides, I have too much fun at my place."

"Why'd you name it Charlie's Heart?" she asked.

He looked down at his plate as though he was uncomfortable. "Because it's important to me, I guess, a dream I had when I was slogging after runaway heifers in the rain."

"It was a nice dream," she said, forking up a bite of ozo. "And a great place."

"Thank you." He smiled warmly, making her breath catch.

"I told you about my parents' accident and my aunt," she said, recovering enough to swirl up the last of her entrée—jumbo shrimp and gorgonzola cheese in a cream and white wine sauce that made a person want to dive in and lick the bowl. "Does it bother you to talk about your parents?"

The question hung there like an uninvited guest, while he speared the last bite of his beef tenderloin capped with shallots and mushrooms. While he chewed, he took off his tie and tucked it into his inside jacket pocket.

Watching his tanned fingers free the top two buttons of his shirt had to be one of the most tantalizing things Robin had ever seen. She wanted to fan herself with her napkin.

"Fair enough question," he said after he'd pushed aside his empty plate, blotted his mouth and taken a sip of his water.

He folded his arms on the edge of the table and leaned forward. "I can tell you that my old man was as tough as a buzzard, and he didn't cut us any slack just because we were kids, but he had his reasons for the way he was."

"Reasons?" Robin prompted him gently.

"Cattle ranching has become big business with big problems. For individual ranchers it's survive or fail, that simple. The old man knew we'd have to be tough to hang on to what he'd worked so hard for." Charlie traced a pattern on the tablecloth with one finger. "I think any kindness and love that might have been in him dried up after my mother left." Charlie ducked his head for a minute. "I don't remember what he was like before that, but my brothers said he changed, and not for the better. He was a bitter man."

"What was your mother like?" Robin asked, wanting to know about this part of his life, to understand it.

The waiter swooped over to take their plates and to tempt them with dessert. Robin ordered a sorbet flavored with peaches and champagne, but Charlie settled for coffee. Since he was driving, she was pleased to see that he'd limited himself to one glass of wine.

"I don't usually talk about that woman," he said when the waiter had left. The hostile words were in direct contrast to his flat tone.

Robin reached across the table to cover his hand with hers. "It's okay. Don't worry about it." She ignored her disappointment. After all, there was a big something she didn't talk about either.

"What perfect timing," she added when the waiter reappeared with Charlie's coffee and her sorbet. She shared several bites with him as they talked of inconsequential things.

"Dinner was really wonderful," she told him as they drove back to Waterloo through the twilight.

He captured her free hand in his and raised it to press his warm mouth to the palm. "I'm glad you enjoyed it."

For the rest of the drive home, smooth, lazy jazz spun out from Charlie's impressive stereo system. Despite Robin's growing attraction to the man beside her, she could feel her reservations grow. Conversation faltered and finally died.

"Are you okay?" Charlie asked quietly.

She knew he looked at her, but she didn't turn her head. Instead she forced herself to pat his arm.

"I'm fine."

When they got back to her house, Charlie followed her inside. As she circled the kitchen table, trailing her hand over its surface, he tracked her with his gaze.

"Would you like something to drink?" she asked, breaking the silence that was building like a third presence. "I could make some coffee." She'd bought some beer, too, but it didn't seem like that kind of an evening.

Wearing a brooding expression, he shook his head. "No, thanks." When he approached her, his movements were as smooth as those of a big cat. A predator stalking its intended prey.

Robin shivered, nervously licking her lips as emotions ran through her—anticipation, fear, curiosity, longing.

Charlie's gaze shifted, following the small movement of her tongue, and his eyes darkened to black. When he reached her, instead of pulling her into a passionate embrace, he lifted his hands and gently cupped her face.

Robin wasn't sure that she wanted tender. Maybe she needed to be swept up into a raging river of desire. To find out how far passion could take her before panic replaced it.

Charlie's gaze seemed to bore right through her. He sighed, and then he dipped his head.

His kiss was so sweet that it made her ache. She parted her lips, expecting more, wanting more.

Then he surprised her by lifting his head and pressing his mouth to her forehead. Her eyes flew open.

"I have to go," he said, letting his hands fall to his sides. A muscle jumped in his cheek. "I had a great time."

"I don't understand," she blurted, confused, as he stepped back. "I thought…"

"That I want you," he filled in for her. "Oh, yeah. So much that I'll start kicking myself for this before I even get back to my truck."

"Then why?" she almost wailed. "I'm willing."

He pointed his finger as though he were firing a gun. "I want more." His grin was crooked. "We'll have more. I promise."

Her vision blurred, and she realized she was crying, silent tears that ran down her cheeks.

Shaking his head, he hurried back to her. "No, babe, don't do that." He caught one of her tears on the tip of his finger and touched it to his lips. "We'll work this out, whatever it is. I'm not disappointed, okay?" Again his grin flashed. "Well, maybe a little."

"I don't understand," she said again.

"My gut tells me you aren't ready. It's too important to rush, that's all." He shoved his hands into the pockets of his slacks and rocked back on his heels. "You can trust me, you know."

Before she could think of a reply, he spun around and crossed the kitchen. Pulling open the door, he went through it, as though he needed air.

Robin watched from the window. He looked so handsome in that suit, with the glow of the streetlight on his bare head. He opened the door to his truck and then he looked up. Hesitantly, she waved, wondering what he really thought.

He blew her a kiss in return, just as though nothing was wrong.

She hoped he meant it. Especially the part about her being able to trust him. There were things she needed to say to Charlie, and she needed to say them soon.

Chapter Ten

He'd been right about regrets, Charlie thought as he drove away from Robin's house. Already part of him wished he'd stuck around to see what developed between them instead of following his gut instinct—or maybe it had merely been his ego—that wanted her more than *willing*.

He wanted—no, needed, with every fiber inside him—to know she was as hungry, as eager, as desperate for him as he was for her.

Passive, accepting, *willing* just damn well wasn't enough. Not this time and not with this woman.

Charlie slapped his hand against the wheel as he went back over the evening's events in his mind. Dinner had gone fine, he was sure of it. The restaurant was always reliable. The conversation had flowed. Robin had been relaxed, even flirtatious, as awareness simmered between them.

He sure as heck was experienced enough to know when a woman was interested.

Driving back to Waterloo after dinner, she'd gotten quiet. He had assumed she was tired. When he walked her into her kitchen, she'd seemed a little spooked, but he'd chalked it up to anticipation.

Nervous about the idea of becoming intimate with someone for the first time. For a man it was simple: am I prepared, am I reading her signals right, will I please her, what about consequences?

For a woman, it had to be even harder: is it too soon, will he still respect me, will he come back around if I say no? If the magazine he'd read in the doctor's office told the truth, a woman also worried about "Will he think my boobs are too small or my butt's too big?"

What he'd seen in Robin's eyes tonight had gone past all that. Until she trusted him enough to level with him, he'd wait.

And probably go crazy in the meantime. Or die of pneumonia from all the time he figured on spending in cold showers.

After Charlie left, Robin tossed and turned for a long time. When she was finally able to sleep, it seemed like her alarm went off only moments later.

"The doc got called over to the Carter place out

past Elizabeth,'' Erline announced the moment Robin walked into the clinic. ''There was an emergency with their daughter's horse.''

Robin set down her purse, wishing she'd stopped for a latte at the drive-through.

Erline handed her a message. The other woman's nails, Robin noticed, were painted with rainbow stripes to match her blouse. ''Paul Bassett's called twice about that heifer you treated. Asked if you'd get back to him first chance you have.''

Robin stared down at the piece of paper without touching it. A headache nagged at her temples, and the day was sliding downhill fast.

''Hello? Is there a problem?'' Erline asked, waving the slip of paper in front of Robin's face.

She nearly snatched it out of the receptionist's hand. ''No, of course not. I was just trying to remember my chart notes.'' She glanced down at Erline's neat handwriting without reading a word of it. ''Do you have the file handy?''

Erline's jaw worked her gum as she extended the folder. ''You look tired, Doc. Late night?''

Robin forced a smile. ''I didn't sleep very well, that's all.'' If she mentioned having dinner with the sheriff, Erline's fertile imagination would draw its own conclusions.

''How's Wyatt?'' Robin hoped a change of subject would distract the other woman. ''He seems really nice.''

The tactic worked all too well, as Erline launched

into a detailed description of their weekend together on the carnival rides, dancing at Charlie's place and watching the rodeo. When she started talking about bringing Wyatt back to her place, Robin could take no more.

"I'd better follow up on this," she said, pointing to the file. "I'm glad you had such a good time."

She didn't need to review her notes on Paul Bassett's cow. She remembered everything about that night, right down to her overreaction to his undoubtedly innocent drink offer.

Biting her lip, she glanced down at his number and reached for the phone. Briefly she considered stalling until Doc Harmon got back and asking him to fill in for her, but what explanation could she give? Rechecking a suture was hardly beyond her scope of experience. Anything else would make her look like a hysterical female instead of a competent professional.

Not the image she was going for.

Doc Harmon had been good to her, and she didn't want him to think he'd made a mistake in hiring her. Her past wasn't his problem. What she needed was to put Brian's memory behind her and move on.

Feeling better after her pep talk, Robin dialed the number. A woman answered and asked Robin to wait while she fetched her husband.

When he came on the line, Robin identified herself and inquired about the cow.

"That place you sewed up don't look like it's healing very good,'' he replied. ''I think you should come back out.''

''Can you describe the problem?'' she asked, grabbing a pen and a notepad.

There was a long pause. ''I'm only trying to do you a favor here.'' He'd lowered his voice. ''To give you a chance to put things right.''

A chill ran through Robin. Had she done something wrong, made a mistake, just because she'd been uncomfortable?

''I guess I could be there in a half hour,'' she replied.

''I'm going to be busy the rest of the day,'' he said hastily. ''You'll have to make it after six. Come straight to the barn, just like last time.''

Robin nibbled on her lip while she looked through her appointments. ''I could check on the animal this morning and give you a report when it's convenient.'' How serious could the problem be if he was willing to let it go all day? ''Or you could call my cell phone.''

''No, that don't work. The dogs go nuts when I'm not home. They don't like strangers coming around, and my wife really can't handle them alone.''

Robin felt sorry for his wife. The situation was beginning to sound like a difficult one.

''Maybe I should just call the regular vet,'' Bassett continued when she didn't respond, ''and see how he wants to handle this.''

Robin still wasn't sure what *this* was, but she fig-

ured Doc Hanson would expect her to make some
attempt to deal with it herself. The cow must not be
in imminent danger or Bassett wouldn't want her to
wait.

"I guess I'll see you at six," she agreed.

"At the barn, like before." The reminder was followed by a click. He'd hung up.

Robin made a face at the receiver. Too bad she
couldn't add a surcharge to her bill for dealing with
a jerk.

"Thanks, Roy, I appreciate your help." Charlie
flipped his notebook shut and shook the older man's
hand.

"I knew something was fishy by the way they was
dressed. Wish I'd thought to get a license number,"
the other man said regretfully as he walked Charlie
back to his Jeep.

"No reason for you to. What you told me is terri-
fic." Charlie finished the coffee Roy had insisted on
giving him. "Give me a call if you see anything else
even a little bit unusual, would you? Even if it doesn't
seem important."

"Sure thing," Roy replied. "Killing stock's a
shameful business, and your brothers have always
been good neighbors." He narrowed his eyes and
leaned closer. "Who do you think is behind it?"

Charlie shrugged. "I can't comment on an ongoing
investigation, but I'll let you know when I can."

Roy held up a detaining hand. "I understand, Sheriff. Just catch the sons of guns, okay?"

I intend to, Charlie muttered to himself after he'd left Roy's and headed down the road to his old homestead. He just didn't have a lot to go on yet—two men dressed as though they were heading for a line dance competition, in fancy, Western shirts and blue jeans, changing a tire on a white sedan, probably a rental car, on the same day the last dead cattle had been found.

It was slim, but it was something.

Now if figuring out Robin's puzzle would be as simple. He'd wanted to call her this morning, to reassure himself she was all right, but he'd forced himself to hold off and give her some time. Some breathing space.

He glanced at his watch. She'd had time enough, he decided. No reason he couldn't go by the clinic on his way back to the station.

Moments later he pulled up out front. There was only one car parked there, and it wasn't Robin's tan Rabbit.

It was too late to turn back, so he went inside.

"I'm sure she'll be disappointed to hear that she missed you," Erline told him after she'd explained that Robin had calls all afternoon. "You two sure heated up the dance floor when we came in with my friend Carol." Sighing dramatically, she patted her heart with the flat of her hand. "Talk about pure poetry, just like those ballroom dancers I've seen on TV.''

Charlie leaned over her desk and lowered his voice, even though the office was empty except for the two of them and an unhappy cat confined the back room. ''I never got the chance to thank you properly,'' Charlie said. ''I don't think Robin would have been willing to come down to the club at all if you hadn't brought her along with you.''

''Don't you worry,'' Erline replied. ''That coupon you slipped me for the two free dinners was payment enough. Besides, I never would have considered doing it if I hadn't known she'd enjoy herself once she got there.''

It was Erline's turn to lean closer, giving Charlie a glimpse of the impressive curves that were barely covered by the scooped-out neckline of her striped blouse. He took a look, knowing she expected it. From his reaction, either his testosterone level was down a quart or his interest was fixated on someone else.

Charlie's money was on answer B.

''Robin looked awfully sleep deprived when she got here this morning,'' Erline continued with a knowing smirk. ''You wouldn't have anything to do with that, would you?''

It hadn't been late when he'd left Robin's house. If she'd been called out, Erline would know.

''I'm afraid I can't take the credit.'' He gave Erline

a conspiratorial wink. "Perhaps she stayed up too late watching a movie," he suggested, "or reading."

Erline snorted and rolled her eyes. "Yeah, right."

Charlie leaned on the counter between them. "You do know I'd be after you like beer chases whiskey, don't you, if I thought I had a chance?"

Erline laughed loudly and slapped the top of the desk with her palm. "Shut up!" Her cheeks turned pink. "You're lucky I've got a phone to answer, or I'd show you what handcuffs are really for," she replied.

"Really?" Charlie was intrigued. Perhaps he could persuade Robin... Uh-uh. Don't go there.

He snapped his fingers. "Darn. And me with crooks to catch, so there you go."

"I'll tell Robin you were here," she said.

He thanked her as he left, the smile stuck firmly to his face until he was back in his Cherokee, but he couldn't help wondering if Robin's insomnia was because of anything he'd done—or not done.

A bank of ominous, rumbling thunderclouds had gathered on the horizon like a dark stain by the time Robin left the drive-in where she'd stopped for a bite on her way to her six-o'clock appointment. The wind whipped across the road, stirring up the dust and dry grasses of late summer, and the sky had a brittle glow, as though the air around her was charged with electricity.

Every few minutes, lightning crackled against the

scowling, towering purple backdrop, adding another layer of tension to Robin's already strained nerves.

She was no fan of storms, especially those that boomed overhead and made her nerves jump. Add that to her worry that she'd overlooked something in treating Bassett's heifer and her disappointment that she'd just missed Charlie.

When her headache returned, starting with a vicious stab of pain that settled into a dull, throbbing presence, she wasn't even surprised. It had been that kind of day.

Doc Harmon had come back right after lunch, his worn face wearing the kind of grim expression that told its own story.

"I hate it when all we can do is end an animal's suffering," he growled. He'd gone on to tell Robin that the horse he'd seen that morning was a wobbler he'd first diagnosed just a few weeks earlier.

Robin knew from her studies that when an afflicted horse or dog suffered from the chronic, progressive disorder, probably caused by a spinal deformity, there was no cure and surgery was seldom an option. Once an animal lost its coordination, there was only one choice, and Doc's sad duty had been to convince the heartbroken teenage owner that the time had come.

All Robin had been able to do was to pat his arm, before she'd left for a couple of appointments. She'd returned to the clinic right before an elderly man wearing a shabby brown suit brought in his equally ancient rottweiler. The dog moved with obvious pain and had, according to its chart, been getting steadily worse.

The frail, stooped old man was as resigned as a loving owner could ever be. His hand shook as he gave the leash to Robin.

"I want to stay with Marcus until the end," the man said in a voice that cracked.

While Robin was examining the old dog, he had licked her hand, and she'd had to swallow hard to keep the tears from forming. Only the certainty that the slightest sign of emotion from her would have shattered the poor owner's shaky composure had kept her from losing control.

Now she clamped her hands on the steering wheel and focused on the situation ahead of her as she eased her car from the main road into Bassett's driveway and was greeted by the same bunch of dogs as the last time she'd been here. None of them looked like poor Marcus, but somehow their protective instincts, combined with her lack of sleep the night before, had her fighting tears once more.

Now was not the time for preoccupation.

When she drove past the house that looked even shabbier in daylight than it had the other night, she noticed that the car she'd seen parked by the door when she'd been here last was nowhere around. Despite the gloom of the clouds, the windows of the house were all dark.

It looked like Mrs. Bassett had gone out.

This time when Robin pulled up by the barn, a

younger man came out to meet her. He needed a shave and a clean set of clothes, but his smile was friendly enough.

"We been waiting for you," he said, hands stuck into his jeans pockets. "Come on."

Robin followed him inside, where the rancher stood by the same stall as before. Thunder cracked overhead, but Robin managed not to flinch. After he'd greeted her, he sent the younger man away.

"Go get yourself some supper, Mel. I'll catch up with you later," he said gruffly.

Robin had already opened the stall door so she could examine the stitches. Although the incision appeared a little infected, she didn't think it was from anything she hadn't done, nor did it really warrant another visit from her.

She turned to tell Bassett that, in case he assumed she'd come back for free. Without her notice, he'd sneaked up behind her to stand so close that she nearly bumped into him.

"Oh, I didn't hear you," she exclaimed, pressing one hand to her heart.

His gaze followed the movement, making her wish she was wearing coveralls over her knit top.

There was no room for her to back up. "Excuse me," she said. "I need to get my bag."

For a moment she didn't think he was going to move, but finally he blinked and stepped back. Trembling, she left the stall.

When she was back in the aisle, she took a deep

breath and reached for the control that was slipping away. "Did you try to treat the sore yourself?" she asked.

"I've been too busy," he replied. "Mel just noticed it today. She's a great little breeder. I'd hate to lose her."

Robin reminded him of her previous instructions. "I'm not saying you shouldn't have called me," she added, making sure that her tone of voice didn't convey disapproval. "But I will have to charge you for today's visit."

"We all have to make a buck when we can," he drawled.

Through the open doorway, Robin glimpsed a flash of lightning. While she was getting what she needed from her bag, thunder boomed again. Louder, like a warning.

Paul was watching her closely. "Storms bother you?" he asked.

"Not at all," she lied.

He shifted so she had to brush past him to get back into the stall. She sucked in her breath and leaned away.

"They sure bother me. If I get scared, I might just have to jump right into your arms," he said.

Robin gritted her teeth and forced herself to give his overweight body a long look. "I don't think that would be a good idea."

He slapped his leg and laughed loudly, as though she'd said something hilarious, but his outburst sounded forced. She was eager to finish up and get away. The thunderheads stacked high and dark outside felt less threatening than the atmosphere in the barn. The intensity of Bassett's stare was unnerving.

Robin bit her lip and went to work.

After she'd cleaned the area carefully and given the cow an injection, she saw a rough patch on its hock. She bent down for a closer look. The spot was just dried mud, but she felt something brush across her backside.

Startled, she straightened. Once again, Paul was standing too close.

"Is there a problem?" he asked, his expression innocent. Had he accidentally rubbed against her or was his touch deliberate?

Robin couldn't be sure. "No." She swallowed her frustration. "No problem, but I need a little more room here.

"Oh, sure." He made a show of stepping back. "That enough?"

Another roll of thunder exploded overhead. This time Robin was unprepared and she flinched.

"I thought you didn't mind storms," he said with a smirk.

"I thought you did!" she shot back.

He shrugged, scratching at his double chin with dirty fingernails. "We could wait it out in the tack room," he suggested. "There's a cot. And that whiskey you turned down last time."

The blatancy of his suggestion made Robin's jaw drop. "What about your wife?" she blurted.

He must have taken her question as an indication of interest in his proposition, because he shifted closer and put one beefy hand on her shoulder. "It's her bridge night." His smile didn't reach his eyes. "She'll be gone for hours."

Before Robin could protest, he pushed her against the side of the stall. "Come on." His voice was hoarse, sending a shiver through her.

Reason said he wouldn't dare cross the line, not right here in his barn. Reason warned her not to over-react and look foolish.

"Touch me again, and I'll scream," she threatened as fear sent adrenaline pumping through her. This couldn't be happening, not again. She wouldn't let it.

He chuckled, a dirty sound. "There's no need for that. I'm just trying to be friendly."

Robin pushed past him, and he didn't resist. When he started to follow her out of the stall, she stabbed her finger at him.

"Stay right there, or I swear I'll file a complaint," she said in a low, angry voice.

He raised his hands in mock surrender. "Don't get your knickers in a twist, girlie," he said with a sneer. "I didn't mean anything."

Robin was shaking with reaction as she grabbed her bag. She had to get out of there; she'd mail him the damn bill.

By the time she got outside, the sky had darkened

even more despite the early hour, and the wind whipped around her. Bassett hadn't bothered to follow her, but her hand was shaking and she fumbled with the door. She finally got it open and tossed her bag onto the seat as another deafening roll broke overhead. It was followed by a torrent of hailstones that beat down on her and her car.

"Just what we damn well didn't need right now," Adam muttered from the open doorway of the stable where he and Charlie stood together watching the hailstones bounce against the ground. Adam's expression was grim. "It won't help the haying."

"Does the weather ever cooperate?" Charlie had come by to update his brother on the lead he'd obtained from Roy Newman and the report he'd locked in his home safe.

"Guess not." Adam pulled a bag of chocolate candies from his pocket and offered them to Charlie, who declined. "I heard back from Ed Johnson's niece the other day," Adam said, tossing back a few candies.

"Oh, yeah?" As Charlie took a swig of the bottle of root beer he was holding, it took him a moment to recall the significance of why Adam had contacted her. "So you really think our former neighbor had a bigger reason than just plain cussedness for not wanting his land to fall into your greedy, undeserving mitts?"

Adam aimed a punch with no real force behind it

and tapped him lightly on the arm. "You forgot *grasping.*"

"Yeah, that too," Charlie agreed as he took another swallow of soda. "And avaricious."

Adam's wife, Emily, had bought the parcel that nearly cut the W in two from old Ed Johnson before she'd ever met Adam. Johnson had made her promise not to sell it to the Winchesters. She had agreed, partly to humor the old man and partly because she hadn't planned on marrying again. Johnson hadn't explained his reasons for the bizarre request, and she hadn't asked.

When Adam tracked his former neighbor down in an assisted living facility in Santa Fe, Johnson had refused to see him. After Johnson passed away, Adam had approached the old man's sole remaining heir, who had agreed to watch for clues in her uncle's papers.

Adam hooked his thumb into his belt. "Why would Johnson go to all the trouble of listing his place with an out-of-state broker, when he knew he'd get the best price if he sold it to us? Why did he ask Emily to make him that promise?" His brow was furrowed beneath the brim of his hat. "Did I tell you that Johnson and our folks were classmates?"

"Everyone in Waterloo went to school together, unless they moved here from somewhere else," Charlie interjected. "That doesn't prove anything."

Adam frowned. "But Ed Johnson and our old man

were best friends all through school. So what happened to change that?''

Charlie shrugged. ''It was all a long time ago,'' he said. ''What does it matter anymore? You married Emily and ended up with the land.''

Adam's thoughtful frown turned into a scowl, and he made a threatening move toward Charlie, who held up both hands to ward him off.

''Whoa, now.'' Charlie realized that he'd pushed his older brother's hot button. ''Calm down, bro. No one thinks that's why you married her, at least not anymore.''

Adam wasn't easily riled, but Charlie didn't figure it was a good time to ask if he'd convinced his wife of that yet. Charlie figured if she'd believed the rumors, she would never have married Adam.

''Take it easy,'' Charlie said instead, watching Adam carefully. ''Tell me what you found out.''

Adam glared at him for another moment, and then the tension drained from his bunched muscles and he straightened.

''I didn't learn a thing,'' he growled, obviously disgusted. ''Johnson's niece said there was nothing in his belongings to explain his attitude.''

''Do you believe her?'' Charlie asked.

''Why would she lie?''

Charlie patted his older brother's shoulder. ''Sorry to hear it. Guess that mystery is going to stay unsolved,'' he said. ''Unlike the question of your dead cattle.''

"Did you find out who was doing it?" Adam demanded.

"Not exactly," Charlie replied.

The storm had let up and the hailstones were quickly melting in the sun. In the distance the dark clouds were retreating. Briefly Charlie hoped that Robin had been home during the storm, safe from any fender benders it might have caused. He was surprised that his cell phone hadn't started ringing with accident reports.

Maybe everyone had learned to drive safely and observe the posted speed limit. Maybe he'd be elected the next governor of Colorado.

"Has that outfit that's been trying to buy the ranch contacted you again?" Charlie asked.

Adam scratched his chin. "As a matter of fact, I just got a letter from their attorney. He just wanted to let me know they're still interested, but they won't be upping their previous offer." He fished a few more candies from the bag and rolled them around in the palm of his hand, like marbles. "Maybe they've reached their limit."

"Or maybe they figure something else will happen to change your mind about selling to them," Charlie suggested. He finished off the last of his root beer and set the empty bottle into a recycling bin by the door.

Adam's eyes narrowed. "Something like dead cattle?"

Charlie shrugged. "Could be."

"Was your friend able to find out anything?" Adam asked.

Charlie was tempted to make his brother plead with him a little more before he said anything, but the news was too interesting to withhold.

"If a person knows where to dig, they might find several incidents that could be viewed as suspicious circumstances surrounding buyouts and land grabs connected with our buddies. Nothing concrete enough to be proven in a court of law, but a clear indication that killing a few cattle might not lie beyond the realm of their business practices."

"That's interesting." Adam looked thoughtful. "Now what?"

"Spread the word for everyone to keep their eyes open and to call me if they see anything, and I do mean *anything,* suspicious."

"Will do. Is that all?" A muscle jumped in Adam's cheek. "Do you think anyone here might be in danger? Would they try to hurt my family?"

Charlie swallowed against a sudden lump that rose into his throat. "There's no indication that they've ever crossed that line, or even come close," he replied. "We're talking unethical business practices, okay? Petty stuff, vandalism, sabotaging equipment, one incident of an implied threat, but nothing that was ever carried out." Charlie dredged up a grin. "We'll catch the people doing this, okay? Until we do, just be careful."

"Thanks, bro," Adam said. "It helps knowing you're watching my back."

"Damn straight." Unable to stop himself, Charlie threw his arms around Adam and gave him a bear hug. He wasn't surprised when Adam returned it, clapping Charlie on the back before they both broke away to stare awkwardly at the toes of their respective boots.

As if the timing had been planned, Charlie's cell phone rang, interrupting the necessity to say anything more.

Chapter Eleven

By the time Robin got home from her disastrous visit to Paul Bassett's ranch, her anger had been replaced with a slew of questions and self-doubts that circled inside her head like sharks. Did she wear a label that said "victim"? Was she putting out some kind of signal that was picked up by men like Bassett and Brian?

She unlocked her side door, pretending not to notice Mae's friendly wave from her backyard and then feeling guilty after she'd shut the door behind her. Rubbing her hands together, Robin considered brewing a cup of tea to warm the chill that had spread inside her, but heating water seemed like a lot of trouble. Even turning on the lights required too much effort, so she sat down on the couch in the dark and folded her arms over her bent head.

She knew that second-guessing was a waste of time, but she couldn't help going back over what had happened in Bassett's barn. Had she somehow, without realizing, encouraged him? In the same way she must have misled Brian?

She pressed her fingers to her temples, as though she could squeeze the answers from her brain, but they refused to come.

She was still sitting there, getting nowhere, when she heard a knock on the door. It was probably Mae. Just to be sure, Robin tiptoed to the kitchen and peeked through the doorway. Mae's hair was a blur of white through the window.

Biting her lip, Robin sneaked back into her living room and closed the blinds. She didn't feel like talking to anyone right now. What she wanted was a bath, as soon as she could summon the energy to turn on the taps. Part of her understood that she was over-reacting to what had turned out to be an unpleasant confrontation. She'd been lucky, but it was over.

Robin didn't know how long she'd been sitting on the couch in the dark, listening to the sounds of the neighborhood settling down for the night, when she heard footsteps thump up the back porch.

She held her breath and waited. This time the knocking was much firmer than Mae's had been. She dug her fingers into the couch cushion. Whoever it was knocked again, waited and tried the door, rattling the knob.

She took a deep breath, glad she always locked it.

She heard a thud, as though a hand had thumped the door in frustration, and she considered calling the sheriff's office. Burglars didn't knock first, did they? Besides, those men had been caught.

She nearly jumped out of her skin when someone tapped on the porch window.

"Robin! Are you in there?"

It was Charlie's voice. The burst of relief was replaced by dismay as she sneaked back to the kitchen, feeling like a criminal in her own house. Perhaps she should answer the door, since he was being so insistent, but she didn't want to deal with anyone, not even him. She didn't want to hide her feelings and pretend that nothing had happened or answer his probing questions.

She listened, ears straining, breath burning her lungs. Finally she heard what she'd been waiting for. His footsteps retreated.

Silently, carefully she moved across the darkened kitchen. She nearly fell over the empty laundry basket she'd left by the table, stopping her fall by grabbing at a chair as she swore.

She heard voices outside, Charlie's and Mae's. Stealthily Robin set the basket on the table and went to the window.

Mae was talking as she pointed at Robin's house. Ed was with her. Charlie had his hands on his hips and his head tilted toward her as he listened. Ed was nodding thoughtfully, but Robin couldn't make out their words.

Without warning, Charlie turned to look straight at the window where she stood. Panicked, Robin dropped to the floor. As she began crawling on her hands and knees, the utter irony of the situation hit her. Hysterical laughter bubbled up into her throat, but she pressed her lips together and got to her feet.

Too bad if he saw her. She hadn't called him.

As she passed the wall phone in the kitchen, it rang shrilly, startling her so badly that she almost screamed. Still shaking, she leaned against the counter and waited for the answering machine to take the call.

"Robin, it's Charlie," said the forceful voice. "I know you're there, so pick up the phone if you're okay." There was a pause and the sound of his breathing. "Mae called me. She saw you come home, and she got worried when you didn't answer the door."

Robin stood frozen, unable to decide what to do. She couldn't let them worry about her, but still…

"Robin," he said again, "if you don't answer, so help me, I'm going to break down the door."

When she picked up the phone, Charlie's knees nearly gave out beneath him. The thought had crossed his mind, right after he threatened to force his way in, that breaking down the door might not be too smart.

What if she wasn't alone? What if someone had been waiting for her when she got home and was now holding her hostage? Damn, but he'd had no training for that kind of situation.

"It's me." She spoke barely above a whisper, sending his heart tumbling to his feet. "I'm okay. I just have a headache, that's all." He heard her swallow. "Tell Mae that I apologize for worrying her, okay? And I'm sorry that you came over for nothing. I'm just going to take some aspirin and go to bed."

Before she could break the connection, he cut in. "Robin? Don't hang up, okay?" His brain was racing, trying to think what to do. "You're going to have to open the door, honey, so I can see that you're really all right."

Was he making things worse? Was he putting her in danger? Hell, he had no idea. All he could do was follow his instincts and trust his gut.

He prayed for wisdom and courage. When he saw her face, he hoped he'd be able to tell if anything was really wrong.

His fingers tightened on his cell phone. Mae had insisted that she saw Robin come home alone. Wouldn't he feel like a prize jackass if she'd been mistaken and Robin had company? Male company.

If that was the case, Charlie could just go out and shoot himself with his own gun. It would probably be

a lot quicker and less painful than dying of embarrassment.

"Okay," Robin agreed, "Come back to the porch,
and I'll open the door."

Before he could reply or think how to give her any
kind of secret signal, just in case someone else was
listening, she hung up.

"Wait here," he told Mae, wishing he could send
her home and eliminate a potential witness to his humiliation. Hell, he'd sacrifice his pride in a moment,
he realized, if it meant that Robin was okay.

"Should I get my gun?" Mae whispered.

Charlie grabbed her arm, as frail as a twig beneath
the sleeve of her bright-orange jacket. "No!" he exclaimed, biting off the expletive that nearly followed.
"Please, just stay put."

"Okay, but you don't have to shout," she said, her
tone taking him back to the classroom.

He thought about calling in some backup, but he
rejected the idea. As he climbed the porch steps, his
heart was thumping so loudly he thought it might
jump out of his chest.

He'd been in a few dangerous situations since he'd
taken the job as sheriff, but nothing as bad as the
feeling he'd had when Mae had called to ask if he'd
check on Robin. He'd been working late, stuck at his
desk, getting caught up on the paperwork stacked in
his basket, when her call came in.

Now Robin opened the door a crack and looked
out as fresh worry assailed him. He strained to see

beyond the door. Did someone have a gun to her head? What kind of sheriff was he, if he couldn't even protect the woman he cared for?

''Are you all right?'' he asked hoarsely.

She nodded. ''Yeah, like I said, I just have a head-ache.'' Her face was pale, and there were dark patches under her eyes. ''Can I go now, Sheriff, or were you going to haul me in?'' Her tone hinted at her normal spirit, but it was definitely diluted.

''I'm afraid not, sweetie.'' He jammed the toe of his boot into the opening of the door so she couldn't shut it. ''I'd better take a look around inside, just to reassure myself that everything is really all right.''

''Don't you believe me?'' Her voice had risen, the strain more evident.

In her agitation, she'd let the door open wider. When he saw her, he knew with a sinking feeling that everything wasn't okay.

She looked the way a person did when they'd got-ten bad news—kind of stunned.

''Honey?'' Keeping his voice gentle, Charlie wrapped his hand around the edge of the door to brace it and hoped like hell she wouldn't slam it shut on his fingers.

''Oh, all right.'' Sounding downright grumpy, she flung the door wide open. ''Come on in. Bring the neighborhood, and we'll have a party.'' She turned her back and stalked into the darkened kitchen, leav-ing him no choice but to trail along after her. Before he went into the house, he turned and gave Mae, who was still waiting, a big thumps-up. Hopefully, she wouldn't get a bazooka.

She waved and headed back to her house, while he heaved a sigh of relief.

When he looked back around, Robin had flipped on the light, temporarily blinding him. His reflexes kicked in and he reached for his gun, stopping himself by curling his hand into a fist.

Robin was blinking against the brightness. "Since when is wanting to be alone a crime?" she demanded, arms folded protectively across her chest.

Charlie wasn't sure what was going on, so he didn't come any farther into the kitchen. "I stopped by the clinic to say hi, but you were out on a call," he said.

Her nod was shaky. "I heard." She chewed her lip. "Sorry I missed you."

He felt as though someone had shoved him right back to square one with no explanation. "So how are you?" he asked, feeling his way slowly.

"Fine." Her chin went up defensively.

He waited, but she didn't say anything else. "I wish I didn't have to intrude," he said, puzzled by her manner, "but I need to look around. Is that a problem?"

She hitched one shoulder in a lopsided shrug and stepped aside. "Help yourself."

He drew his weapon and did a search, surprised when he was finished that she hadn't moved.

"All done," he said, holstering his gun. "I hope you understand why I had to do it."

"Yeah." Her head was bowed, and she didn't bother to raise it enough to make eye contact. Something weird was definitely afoot, but he had no clue as to what.

His frustration boiled over, and he hauled her into his arms. Only then did she look up, clearly startled, as he bent his head and kissed her.

She remained motionless as he used every bit of skill he had in an attempt to get a response from her. Then, just as he was about to give up, she wrapped her arms around his neck and kissed him back.

Why they didn't burn her house down with the scorching heat they generated, he had no idea. All he knew, before his brain stopped working, was that no other woman had ever stirred him like the bundle of dynamite he held in his arms right now. If she had asked him to make love with her in the middle of Nugget Street, he would have happily complied.

Her tongue was tangled with his in a hot, wet dance of desire, her hands grabbed and stroked every part of him she could reach, and her tight little body rubbed against his arousal until he doubted he could get her to the bedroom fast enough.

Hell, both of them were still fully dressed. Charlie managed to open his eyelids just enough to see if there was anyplace besides the floor to lay her down and crawl on top of her. What he saw instead were tear tracks running down her cheeks.

He jerked away from her so fast that she stumbled

forward, but he braced himself as he caught her by the shoulders.

"What's the matter?" he demanded. Had he been too rough? She was such a little thing. Had he hurt her? Shame washed over him.

He was hoping for absolution, for some explanation he could accept without feeling lower than a junkyard dog.

"Nothing! Why does anything have to be wrong?" Her voice was brittle, her cheeks flushed with, he hoped, passion matching his own.

"You're crying," he shouted, frustrated. "It's not the response I was going for."

She scrubbed her cheeks with her hands and then she spun around so her back was to him. "Would you just leave?" she asked.

Charlie was stunned. Had he scared her? "Look," he said, fumbling his way. "I'm sorry if I came on too strong. I never meant—"

"Please," she repeated in a quavery voice. "I'm embarrassed enough. I'd like you to go."

"I can't leave you like this," he protested. "You're too upset. I swear I won't touch you again, if you don't want me to, but let me stay until you're okay."

She straightened her shoulders and turned around. Tears still leaked from her eyes, but her gaze was steady on his. "I'm fine, really. I'm sorry that I worried you and Mae. I have a headache. I think I'll just take a warm bath and go to bed." Her chin went up in a gesture that was becoming familiar. "If I gave you the wrong idea, I apologize."

Charlie took a step forward, and she immediately took a step back. He stopped. "You can talk to me, you know. As a friend. If you aren't ready for more right now. A blind man could see that something has upset you. If it wasn't me, then what?"

Her smile trembled. "It wasn't you."

"Has someone hurt you?" he demanded grimly. "I'll help you through it, whatever you need."

She surprised him by closing the gap between them and reaching up to rest her hand against his cheek. "Thank you." Her voice was husky. "You're a good man. You have a generous heart and a wonderful family." She blinked hard. "Go home. You deserve someone who can make you happy."

He covered her hand with his. "*You* make me happy," he said, "except when I'm worried, like now."

She drew her hand away, and her expression hardened. He knew that he'd lost the argument, at least for tonight, and he wasn't even sure why.

"I'm not giving up," he told her after she'd followed him to the door. "Not yet."

Robin didn't even bother to respond.

She went through the next few days as though a layer of insulation separated her from the rest of the world. She functioned, she even laughed on occasion. She did her job, and when she was done, she went home. Mae had apologized for calling Charlie, and Robin had convinced her not to give it another thought.

"It's a comfort knowing I have neighbors like you," Robin told Mae, handing over the rent check. "It was rude of me to ignore your knock, but I had such a headache."

"I understand, dear," Mae replied, patting her hand. "Nothing deals with that better than a couple of aspirin, a cup of hot tea and a nice bath. I think you work too hard."

"You're probably right," Robin had replied.

Now she stood at the front clinic window congratulating herself for maintaining her emotional equilibrium so well. She'd put the incident with Paul Bassett behind her. If she missed Charlie, no one else suspected. She was sure of it.

Brian was a distant, unpleasant memory. If he had found happiness in his life, maybe in the afterlife he'd burn in hell. One could only hope, but she wasn't going to waste any more time on him.

Then she heard a siren. A sheriff's deputy drove by with his lights flashing, followed by another one, both going fast.

"What was that?" Erline asked, pushing back her chair.

Doc wandered in from the storage room. "Was that the fire truck?" he asked.

Robin shook her head, stomach clenched. "Sheriff's deputies. Two of them."

"Two?" Doc echoed. "Pretty unusual for these parts. I wonder what's going on."

"Maybe a bad accident out on the highway," Erline suggested. "Are you sure you saw two sheriff's cars?"

Robin nodded, her throat tight. What she hadn't seen, though, was Charlie's Jeep. What if he'd been hurt?

"All available units," Charlie radioed, driving as fast as he dared on the winding two-lane road. "I'm following a white sedan headed south on Baxter. We've just passed the old Grange Hall, and we're coming up to the Y with Jefferson. My bet is they're heading for Highway 24." He rattled off the license number of the other car. "Call the state boys," he added. "Let them know what's going on."

"Will do," the dispatcher replied. "Two units headed your way."

Everyone who lived in the area had been asked to report anything unusual. Adam's men patrolled the boundaries of the ranch as best they could, and the livestock had all been moved to pastures away from the road.

This morning the school bus driver had spotted the car Charlie was chasing. When Charlie had attempted to talk to the two men inside, they'd refused to pull over, cranking up the speed instead. Now he was on their tail with full lights and siren.

Up ahead, he knew, was a bad curve. He backed

off a little, hoping the sedan would ease up, as well. He didn't want to endanger anyone who might be coming from the other direction. The passenger in the white car turned around to look at Charlie, but their speed increased.

Briefly Charlie lost sight of them in the curve, but when he came on around, he saw that the driver had lost control. The sedan had slid over onto the dirt shoulder. Dust and gravel flew as the car fishtailed. Charlie slowed even more and radioed his exact location.

"Reggie and Herb are both on their way," dispatch replied. "Estimated time of arrival is less than five minutes."

Just then, the driver overcorrected in his attempt to regain control. The car flipped over, landing upright. Through the dust, Charlie could see the driver hunched over the steering wheel, unmoving.

Charlie jammed on his brakes and slid to a stop. He could hear sirens in the distance. Maybe this would end easily, after all.

He was waiting for backup to arrive when the passenger opened fire. The side window of the Cherokee shattered, and Charlie felt a burning pain in his shoulder.

It was a good thing Robin's appointments this afternoon were all routine. Ever since the deputies had raced by a little while ago, her concentration had been ruined.

What if Charlie was in danger? Even Doc had given up all pretense of concentrating on anything else. He'd headed down to Emma's Café in the hope of finding out what was going on. He'd taken his cell phone with him and promised to call the clinic if he learned anything.

Robin did her best to smile and focus as she escorted a feline patient and its owner from one of the small examining rooms into the reception area. The young bluepoint Siamese with a crook in its tail had come in for a routine checkup. Robin had given the cat its immunizations and drawn blood for the lab tests. Before the owner put the cat back into its carrier, she'd asked Robin to clip its nails.

"Max hates having it done," she'd said apologetically. "I don't want him mad at me."

Neither Max nor his owner had any idea how lucky they were that Robin hadn't accidentally clipped a toe or two as well as his nails, since she'd been too concerned about Charlie to concentrate.

She still went weak at the knees when she thought about the way he'd kissed her, right before she had turned into the ice queen and kicked him out.

"Thank you, Mrs. Adams. Erline will call you with Max's test results." She bent down and scratched his head through the door of his carrier. He purred, so she assumed he held no grudge over the nail clipping.

Robin had done a lot of thinking since Charlie had left the other night. Someone had mentioned a women's shelter over in Elizabeth that had a support group. Maybe it was time for her to give them a call.

There was no one else in the waiting area, except Erline, so Robin poured herself a glass of water and sat down in one of the chairs. When the phone rang, Erline pounced on it like a barn cat on a field mouse. Robin waited anxiously, hoping it was Doc with some news.

Erline looked up and nodded as she listened to the voice at the other end. "How bad?" she asked with a worried frown.

Robin's knuckles turned white around the glass she was holding. Not Charlie, she thought. Feeling immediately selfish, she sent up a wordless prayer for whoever might have been hurt.

She strained to listen, but she couldn't hear a thing. When Erline shook her head, Robin set down her glass and pressed a hand to her heart.

Erline's gaze sought hers again. "Okay, I'll tell her," she said into the phone. "Where did they take him?"

Robin's heart nearly stopped. Oh, God. She got to her feet and ran over to grab her purse as Erline hung up and took a deep breath.

"Is it Charlie? Is he okay?" Robin demanded, but she already knew the answer.

"He was chasing the men who've been killing his brothers' cattle," Erline replied. "There were shots fired. Both Charlie and one of the guys he was chasing were hit."

Robin began trembling, deep in her bones. Tears filled her eyes, but she wiped them away.

"How bad?" she asked hoarsely.

"Doc didn't know for sure, but no one had to be airlifted to Denver or anything like that. It can't be too serious."

"He's been shot!" Robin exclaimed. "That sounds serious to me!"

Erline slid back her chair and came around the desk to give Robin a hug. "It's going to be okay," she said. "He's right here in town at the medical clinic on Pine. Do you know where it is?"

Robin was halfway to the door before Erline was done speaking. As Robin ran to her car, she had no idea if she'd even answered.

When she got to the clinic and hurried inside, she saw a uniformed deputy standing by the counter. Charlie was just walking out of a room. He was shirtless and one shoulder was bandaged. Both he and the doctor with him looked up as Robin approached them. Now that she was here, she had no idea what to say.

"Hi, sweetheart!" A welcoming smile spread over Charlie's face, and he held out his good arm.

The sight of him standing there, more or less in one piece, devastated Robin's defenses. Fresh tears of relief filled her eyes as she rushed to him. He gathered her close in a one-armed hug and buried his face in her hair while she tried to wrap her arms around his waist without doing more damage.

"Are you okay?" she mumbled, her wet cheek pressed against his warm skin. She could hear his heart beating, steady and strong, beneath her ear.

"Yeah, except for one little bitty hole, I'm just fine." His chest expanded as he drew in a long breath. "I'm so glad you're here," he whispered.

For a moment they just held each other. She wished she could just soak him up, right through her pores. Instead she turned her head and touched her lips to the bare skin right above his flat male nipple.

He groaned into her hair, and his arm tightened around her shoulders. "You checking to see if I'm still alive?" he muttered, his voice strained.

"Don't joke about it!" She pulled away from him. "It's not funny."

"Thanks for caring." He leaned down and touched his mouth to hers.

"Sheriff, I can see you're in good hands," the doctor said, holding out some papers. "Follow my instructions and all you'll end up with is a sexy little scar."

After Charlie had introduced Dr. Choe to Robin, the doctor excused himself. "Call me if you have any questions," he said as he left.

When he was gone, Charlie glanced at the deputy and then led Robin over toward the window. "I've got some stuff to take care of," he told her. "And I need to talk to Adam and Travis before someone else does. Can I call you?"

She swallowed, hating to hear the hesitation in his

voice. Who could blame him, though, after all the mixed signals she'd given him.

"I'd like that," she said, touching his cheek. "Those men you were after, did you catch them?"

He nodded. "Sure did. They're locked up."

Robin took a deep breath. "I'd like to talk," she said. "There are a few things I need to explain, if you'll listen."

"Sounds good." This time his smile made Robin feel warm all over.

"Sheriff?" The uniformed deputy who'd been with Charlie when Robin arrived waited by the counter. "Do you want me to take you home now?"

"No, Deputy, you can give me a ride down to the station." Charlie's gaze shifted back to Robin. "Later?" he asked.

"Of course," she replied. "Whenever you feel up to it." Part of her wished she could talk to him right now and put what she had to say behind her. The other part was thankful for the respite. Either way, she knew she would never be free to face the future until she'd dealt with the past.

Chapter Twelve

The next morning Robin decided to treat herself to breakfast out. Her decision was based mainly on the fact that she hadn't taken the time to stop at the grocery store after dropping in at the medical clinic the day before. She'd been too keyed-up about Charlie getting shot to think about anything as mundane as a shopping list.

It was only this morning when she opened the door of the refrigerator that she realized there was nothing there to eat. Unless, of course, one could make breakfast from pepper jack cheese, green onions, an apple with brown spots, a questionable-looking hot dog and sour milk.

Emma's Café did a bang-up breakfast business, but

there were usually a couple of empty places at the counter. When Robin walked in, the café was busy. She glanced around, looking for Erline or anyone else she knew.

She noticed Paul Bassett seated in a booth with three other men. He was looking at her, but she ignored him.

The hostess, an older woman named Marjorie, hurried up to Robin with a menu.

"Maybe you'd like to sit in the back," Marjorie suggested in a low voice. "There's a small table that's empty."

Robin was about to reply that the counter was fine when she realized that a hush had fallen over the room. Several patrons had turned to stare at her.

Had she forgotten to button her blouse?

Before she was able to check, one of the men sitting with Bassett leaned across the table.

"Better hide, Paulie," the man said loudly. "That hot lady vet just might jump you." The men all guffawed, and the one next to Bassett slapped his shoulder.

A few other people giggled and more turned to gape. It took Robin a moment to realize they were laughing at her. Her face went hot, and the comment Bassett's friend had made finally sank in.

The hostess looked at Robin helplessly. "What do you want to do, honey?"

There was sympathy in Marjorie's eyes. Robin had

removed some quills from her dog's muzzle a couple of weeks before, and they'd talked for quite a while.

Robin shifted so her back was to the room. "What's going on?" she asked quietly as the level of conversation climbed back to normal.

Marjorie darted a glance toward the kitchen. Holding the menu up like a shield, she pulled Robin over toward the corner by the coat rack.

"I've never cared for Bassett," Marjorie confided, "and not just because he doesn't tip worth beans." She patted her carefully curled and sprayed hair with her free hand. "He and his cronies meet here a couple of days a week. He's been bragging that you made a move on him."

"What?" Robin gasped. "He said that I initiated a pass?" A man at the counter looked up from his newspaper, so she lowered her voice. "When was this tryst supposed to have happened?"

A frown pleated the hostess's brow below her neatly trimmed bangs. "In his barn."

The scum-sucking weasel!

"And what supposedly happened?" Robin hissed.

"Well, he's been saying that you tried to kiss him."

Humiliation washed over Robin like a douse of greasy, cold water. "It's not true."

"Oh, I didn't believe him, not for a minute," Marjorie assured her as Robin pressed her palms to her burning cheeks. "For one thing he's married, and I could tell right off that you're not the kind of girl who would poach.''

Acid churned in Robin's stomach, and she had to swallow hard. She turned to glare at the four men, who were all watching her with avid interest. One of them blew her a big, smacking kiss, and they started laughing again.

"Anyone with sense would know he's lying," the hostess muttered, "but of course there are always a few idiots who'll believe anything they hear.''

"Well, thanks for filling me in," Robin said, teeth clenched. "Tell your dog his next quill-pickin' party is on the house." Tears burned Robin's eyelids, but she was determined not to cry.

"Well, thank you, sweetheart." Marjorie patted her arm. "I don't imagine you feel like staying. I know my appetite would dry right up if it was me they was gossiping about." Her words weren't much help, but her smile was full of sympathy. "I could fix you up something to go.''

More than anything, Robin wanted to turn tail and run, but if she ever hoped to make a place for herself in this town, she had to hold her head up high. Even if they whispered and smirked, just like before.

She shouldn't have to go through this again!

Stand and fight or cut and run, her aunt used to say. *The choice is yours.*

Cutting out sounded awfully good right now.

The busboy had just finished clearing off a table,

smack in the middle of the crowded room. She took a deep breath and pointed.

"I'd like to sit there." She'd have to walk right by her tormentors.

The hostess's penciled brows lifted, two arcs of astonishment. "You sure? I can still put you in the back, behind the plastic ficus tree."

If Robin's jaw clenched any tighter, it would crack like an egg shell. "No, thanks. The table over there will be just fine."

"Good for you, honey." Marjorie elbowed Robin in the ribs. "And your coffee's on me."

After Robin had taken her seat and given her order to the waitress who scurried up, she realized that in theory, standing up to a bully sounded like a great idea. In actuality, it sucked.

Big-time.

Waiting for her omelet, she stirred cream into her coffee, just to occupy her trembling hands. Bassett was too far away for her to overhear what he and his buddies were saying behind their hands, but their leers and kissing sounds were shredding her nerves and wearing away her composure. If those jerks didn't let up on the torture soon, she would dissolve into tears.

The idea that someone might see her crying and draw the wrong conclusion was enough to turn Robin's humiliation to blazing anger. Another loud cackle from Bassett's table boosted her temper into the red zone.

She pushed back her chair and got to her feet.

"I'll be right back," she told the waitress who had brought over Robin's order.

Heart thudding like a hammer, she squared her shoulders and stalked to the booth where the men were seated. For the second time since she'd come through the front door, Emma's Café fell silent.

"Oh, oh," Bassett crowed, dribbling bits of egg from his full mouth. "Save me, boys."

Robin slapped both palms down on the table, making the coffee mugs jiggle. She leaned toward Bassett until they were nearly nose-to-nose. His eyes widened and his jaw stopped working, which gave her a fleeting jolt of satisfaction.

The only sound in the place came from the radio on the counter.

"I guess she can't take no for an answer," the jerk seated across from Bassett, needing a shave and a bath, whispered loudly.

Robin gave him an icy glare, and he took a sudden interest in his pancakes.

She directed her attention back to the man who had succeeded in resurrecting her self-doubts. "If you're going to tell everyone about our little date in your barn," she drawled loudly, "why don't we get the facts straight about who came on to *whom,* shall we?"

"You cornered him," his buddy blurted. "Paulie told us all about it."

"Do you believe everything Paulie tells you?" she asked.

"Well, not hardly," he replied with a sideways glance at her accuser.

Robin turned back to Bassett. "It's bad enough that you tried to force your married, overweight, middle-aged, repulsive self onto me," she stormed, emphasizing each point with a jab of her finger.

His cheeks turned a dark shade of red as beads of perspiration popped out on his forehead, but he remained mute.

She straightened up, parked a hand on her hip and slowly looked around her. She had the attention of everyone in the place, including a couple of tourists in baseball caps made from beer cans that had been flattened and crocheted together like aluminum granny squares. Even the cook was leaning against the counter with his arms folded.

"What's even worse than sexually harassing me is for you to inflate your limp, pathetic *ego* by lying."

She took a deep breath, trembling all over in reaction to what she'd just done. She was as winded as though she'd run a marathon.

To Robin's surprise, two women got to their feet and applauded. "You go, girl!" shouted one, pumping her fist.

Robin noticed that the waitress was still holding her breakfast order. If Robin tried to eat anything, she'd throw it up. Instead she jerked her thumb toward Bassett.

"Put my order on *his* tab."

When Robin headed for the door, head held high,

she noticed the deputy sheriff she'd met at the medical clinic. He was sitting by the window. When his gaze met hers, he grinned and gave her a sassy salute.

Robin made it all the way to her car and tumbled inside before she burst into tears. Resting her forehead against the steering wheel, she let the tangled feelings of anger and pain flow out from the deepest, most private part of her. The fresh emotions were all mixed up with the ones she'd thought were buried.

Finally, eyes and nose streaming, she took a hiccuping breath and fished around in the glove box for some tissues. As she was mopping up her face, she remembered Bassett's surprise when she'd confronted him, and how ridiculous he'd looked with egg—literally—all over his face.

Robin realized she was smiling, even though her eyelids felt puffed out to twice their normal size. The first step toward putting it all behind her had been a doozy, but now that she'd taken it, she had no intention of stopping until she'd gone the distance.

"That was a great meal." Charlie set his empty plate down on the chrome-and-glass coffee table, wiped his mouth on a paper napkin and sat back on his leather couch. His shoulder throbbed with a dull, steady ache, but he avoided the pain pills that made him groggy. "I'm glad you came over."

For the past few days, his apartment might as well have had a swinging door to accommodate his company. His family and friends, customers from his club, old girlfriends he was still on good terms with and people he hardly knew had brought an endless stream of food, booze, flowers, even cash, which he'd suggested they donate to local charities instead.

He'd have to go back to work just to get some rest.

Now the person he had been the most eager to see was finally seated next to him. He wanted to grab her and never let her go, but that would have to wait until he had two good arms.

He smiled into Robin's big, dark eyes and enfolded her hand in his, hoping like hell that what she intended to tell him wasn't ''Get lost.''

At least she didn't snatch her hand away.

''I read in the newspaper that those men who shot you were working for some big food-processing conglomerate,'' she said. ''Did they honestly think your brothers would sell the ranch just because some of their cattle had been killed?''

Charlie started to shrug, but the twinge from his shoulder reminded him that doing so was still a really *bad* idea.

''Apparently, that's exactly what they figured. It will take a couple of agencies a while to sort everything out, but the guys we caught have implicated several executives.''

''Unbelievable.'' Robin shook her head. ''I'll bet your family is happy that it's finally over and that you're going to be all right.''

''I told Adam he owes me a side of beef,'' Charlie joked. Then Charlie recalled Adam's expression when he'd burst into the station after the shooting. It was the first time Charlie had seen fear on Adam's face since Kim ran away from home.

"Are you getting tired?" Robin asked anxiously, snapping Charlie back to the present. "Perhaps I'd better leave, so you can rest."

"Don't go," he pleaded. "Not yet."

She reached for his empty plate. "I'll just clean up these dishes. I made a peach pie, if you'd like some dessert." If her voice got any perkier, it would shatter. She started to get up, but he tightened his grip on her hand.

"The plates will wait." He could feel a tremor go through her, and his gut knotted with apprehension. "So will the pie."

"Sure you don't want some coffee?" she asked, perched on the edge of the couch with desperation plain on her face. "It will only take a minute to fix."

"Maybe later, with the pie." He shifted so he could look at her more easily.

"Okay." She nibbled at her lower lip, clearly ready to bolt.

Charlie struggled for patience. Finally she sighed, turning her hand to lace her fingers with his.

"Then I guess it's time I tell you what I came to say."

He braced himself as he watched her.

He'd been racking his brain, trying to figure out what it was she was finally going to tell him. Was she married, with a husband and children stashed somewhere? Oh, God, he hoped not. Did she have a criminal record? Not likely. A history of drug abuse? No way.

"I'm here, babe, and I'm all ears." This was a whole lot scarier than looking down the barrel of a gun.

She pressed her trembling lips together and looked down at their joined hands. "I was raped," she said baldly.

Her words drove the air from Charlie's lungs and damn near stopped his heart. For a moment he was speechless with shock. The news was worse than anything he could have imagined.

"I'm so sorry."

This wasn't about him. He dragged in a steadying breath and then the cop in him took over.

"When did it happen?" He fought to keep his voice steady. "Samuel told me what happened at Emma's. Was it Bassett?"

Whoever had done it, Charlie would kill him. Even if it meant giving up his badge, he would hunt the man down and kill him like a dog.

Robin shook her head. "Oh, no," she exclaimed, "no. It didn't happen here. It was a long time ago, when I was in veterinary school back in Illinois."

Her gaze slid away from him. "Brian was a fellow student, popular, well-liked, from an influential family," she recited the litany as though she'd been over it a hundred times before.

"How did it happen?" Charlie asked softly.

"I guess you'd call it date rape. I was surprised when he asked me out, because I wasn't in that crowd. You know, the popular circle."

He knew what she meant. The kind of group he'd always been part of. Charlie held her hand tightly in his, willing her to feel his support. "Go on," he said.

"The details don't matter anymore, but after it happened, I thought it was my fault. I thought that somehow I'd given him the wrong signal, because I was so inexperienced."

A virgin, Charlie figured, his heart aching for her. "In a seminar I took, we learned that a lot of women blame themselves," he said, wanting desperately to put his arms around her, but sensing that she wasn't ready. Perhaps she never would be. "Did you report it?"

"Not at first. I was too embarrassed. Then my best friend told me about the rumors she'd heard, about me being a real party girl. I didn't know what to do, so I talked to my advisor." She sighed. "Brian was questioned, but he said I agreed. It was his word against mine."

Charlie's hand tightened on hers. He could only imagine what she had gone through, especially without family to support her.

Robin chewed at her lower lip. "After that, the rumors got worse. Brian accused me of trying to get even because he'd stopped seeing me." She waved her free hand. "He was so charming. Most of the other students believed him and some even blamed me for trying to make trouble for him.'' Her eyes glistened with tears, and she lifted her shoulders in a helpless gesture. ''I guess some of the others didn't want to take sides, or they just didn't care.''

''You were ostracized,'' Charlie guessed. ''The bastard.''

She pressed her hand to her heart. ''I thought I'd put it behind me, but then Paul Bassett offered me a drink. Of course I refused, but when I went back out there, he made a clumsy pass. After I left, I figured I must be giving off some, I don't know, *vibe,* I guess.''

''Did you think I was picking up the same vibe?'' Charlie hated asking. He didn't want to hear that she lumped him with a creep like Bassett, but he had to know. He was doing his best to understand her feelings.

''I wasn't sure.'' She tried to smile and failed. ''I'm sorry.''

Asked and answered. ''Now what?'' he asked, ignoring the jab of disappointment. ''Where do you and I go from here?''

Something lit up in her eyes, a faint spark, and her mouth relaxed a little.

''You and I?'' she echoed.

He didn't have to think twice. ''Damn right.''

''Well, I've joined a support group over in Elizabeth,'' she confessed. ''After I faced Bassett down in front of half the town, I realized there were a few issues I still needed to deal with.''

''How can I help?'' Charlie asked.

She smiled, but her eyes filled with fresh tears, and this time they spilled over. "Be my friend?"

It was less than he wanted to hear, but he would make it be enough.

For now. But not forever.

Charlie raised their joined hands. "Take all the time you need," he said.

Robin studied her reflection in the full-length mirror fastened to the back of her bedroom door and skimmed her hands down the silky fabric of her strapless sheath. She couldn't remember the last time she'd worn red, but this was a special dress for a special night. As soon as she'd received the invitation to the party celebrating the renaming of Charlie's Heart, she'd gone shopping in Denver.

She'd come home with the dress, a pair of strappy sandals that made her legs look as long as an airport runway, a silly little matching purse, enough cosmetics for a photo shoot and lace panties that would fit in a lipstick tube. All the things she'd avoided since Brian.

For the past two months, Charlie had kept the promise he'd made at his apartment. He'd been the best friend Robin had ever known.

They'd gone riding together. She'd attended the church where he sometimes sang in the choir and gone with him to family dinners afterward. They had talked, about everything and nothing.

He'd told her about his parents, that his mother had

deserted them when Charlie was little. And how guilty he'd felt that he barely remembered her and his brothers missed her so much.

Charlie didn't criticize his father, but Robin had formed her own opinion. The Old Man, as all three brothers called Garth Winchester, sounded to her like a harsh disciplinarian who had never shown his boys the love they so desperately needed after losing their mom.

Robin had told Charlie all about her parents and her aunt. The two of them joked and laughed together. She knew Charlie loved marshmallows and didn't eat veal. He knew about her crush on Dwight Yoakum and her cravings for chocolate. They argued politics and pizza toppings. They both loved to travel and wanted kids.

Somewhere between pepperoni and pineapple, she'd fallen so deeply in love with him that she might never climb back out. She couldn't imagine ever wanting to.

The one thing they hadn't shared, not since before Charlie had gotten shot, was a touch or a kiss or anything else that was an inch past platonic. Robin had no idea whether he was still attracted to her that way. Had he lost interest now that he knew all her flaws, or was he merely waiting for a cue from her?

Tonight she planned to find out. If she didn't sprain her ankle in these shoes or asphyxiate herself with her perfume, it was her turn to make a move.

* * *

Charlie stood under the new sign—"Charlie's" in pulsing red and orange neon—greeting the guests for his private party, fielding questions about why he'd changed the name of his club and searching over the tops of heads for a glimpse of his best buddy.

If he ever again agreed to anything as asinine as being "just friends" with a woman who tied him up in knots, he hoped someone would kick him in the head and knock some sense into him.

For two months Charlie had sat on his hands, kept his lips to himself, made sure his fly stayed zipped and taken enough cold showers to end the drought. He knew Robin's family history as well as his own, and he could probably recite a list of her likes and dislikes from memory, but he had yet to see her naked or even nearly so.

What the hell kind of agreement was that?

"Thanks for coming," he recited for probably the fiftieth time.

He had no idea why he'd decided on a private party, since it appeared he had invited the whole damn town. Despite the warmth of the evening, he'd decided on the same gray Western suit he'd worn when he'd taken Robin to dinner in Sedalia. He hoped it might remind her of a nice evening and that wearing it again didn't somehow jinx tonight.

She'd told him all about the progress she'd been making at her support group. She seemed happier, more relaxed and a lot more confident. She would never know he'd run a check on Brian. If the bastard ever stepped out of line again, so much as a toe, Charlie would know. He'd called in all his favors to make sure Brian would never walk away again.

Charlie'd had his fill of friendship and patience. He was tired of kisses on the cheek and handshakes at the door.

Of *course* he would back off on tonight's plan if moving to the next level made Robin feel pressured at all, but he was hoping she'd at least give him some sign, some tiny little encouragement that he wasn't alone in what he felt. Not that he'd turn down sweaty, mutually satisfying sexual activity if she preferred. If she asked him real nice.

"See you inside," he said again, pressing more flesh. "Have a good time."

Finally there was no one else waiting to come inside. With his heart down in his boots, Charlie trailed after the choir director and his wife.

More people would trickle in all evening, he knew. It was just so damn hard to wait for Robin. Seeing her smile, hearing her voice, absorbing her scent— when he was able to breathe it in without tipping her off—had all become the most important parts of his day.

His backup band was playing when he walked in. A buffet was set up along one side of the room, and people were five deep at the complimentary bar.

Mae and Ed Simms, Robin's neighbors, came up to say hello.

"Did she ride down with you?" Charlie asked them. Maybe she'd slipped by him somehow.

"She was still primping when we left, so she said she'd drive herself," Mae replied.

Still primping? Robin was so pretty she stopped Charlie's breath, but he was reasonably sure she didn't spend a lot of time doing girly things in front of a mirror. What could be holding her up?

As soon as Charlie's assistant manager cum announcer spotted him from the stage, he invited the audience to join him in coaxing Charlie to come up and sing.

He'd never felt less like it in his life, but the round of applause and whistles kept building until he finally gave in.

He had cued the band and was just starting to sing one of his favorite numbers when a buzz went up in the back of the room. He'd performed in enough bars to know better than to expect total silence when he sang, but the hometown crowd usually spoiled him.

While he continued, he tried to see what the fuss was about. Finally a path opened up in the crush of people, and a lone woman moved with confidence straight for the stage. Her size and general appearance reminded him of Robin, but any resemblance ended there.

He felt slightly guilty for being attracted to the woman walking toward him. She was wearing a strapless, lipstick-red dress that moved over her curves like liquid heat, and high-heeled shoes that made a man want to crawl on his belly just to kiss her toes. Her hair was the same raven black as Robin's, but it was fluffier. Her eyes were huge and dark and her lips, when she smiled up at him, were nearly as red as her dress, but even more inviting.

When she stopped at the base of the stage, he realized that he'd forgotten all about the song he'd been singing.

"Hi, Charlie." She spoke in Robin's voice over the sound of the band. "Nice party."

Robin watched the expressions chase each other across Charlie's face as he stood there onstage, so handsome he made her mouth water. Did he remember that he'd worn the same suit when he'd taken her to that Italian place for dinner? He'd probably blocked that disastrous night and her strange behavior right out of his memory.

The walk across the dance floor had been the longest of her life. Surprisingly enough, she hadn't felt nervous, but maybe it was because she'd been concentrating so hard on walking without tripping.

She loved the song Charlie was singing when she arrived. He'd performed the same number the last time she was here. When she'd crossed the dance floor, he'd looked puzzled, as though he didn't even know who she was. Then his voice had trailed off, although the band kept playing, and she was close enough to see his eyes go wide with surprise. It was then she realized he hadn't recognized her until that very minute.

Did she look so different now? She sure felt like a whole new woman—from the inside out.

After she'd said hi and he'd nearly dropped his mike, he'd thrust it at the guitar player, while the other members of the band all looked at each other in confusion. Maybe Charlie's exit from the stage hadn't been planned.

At least most of the crowd had started dancing again, but a few people were still staring at him and Robin. Maybe they'd heard about what had happened at Emma's, and so they were waiting to see what she'd do next.

"Hi," Charlie said when he'd made his way over to her. His gaze swept down her body and finally came back to her face. "You look fantastic."

His expression convinced her that he was telling the truth. "Did you buy that dress just for my party?" he asked.

Robin spun around in a circle so he could get the full effect.

"To some extent for the party," she said after she'd turned around to face him again. "But I also bought it for me. What do you think?"

"If I told you what I'm thinking, I'd probably be breaking the law in half a dozen states." He curved his arm around her and bent his head. "I know you spent a lot of time on your appearance," he said into her ear, "but I have to ask, would you be awfully upset with me if we left right now?"

"Why?" she asked, suddenly concerned. "Don't you feel well?"

"Never better," he replied, "but I don't want to share you with anyone else tonight, that's all."

When Robin searched his face, she noticed something glittering in his eyes that she hadn't seen in far too long. Desire. Dangerous, seductive, heavy-lidded hunger, aimed straight at her.

Suddenly, drawing her next breath became a struggle. Heat bubbled through her veins and sizzled along her nerves. Her gaze was locked on his and she couldn't seem to look away.

"But it's your party," she finally managed to whisper.

"Would you rather I kiss you right here in the middle of the dance floor, the way I've been wanting to for two months?" he asked. His voice was harsh, as though he, too, was having trouble speaking. "Because, honey, I guarantee that unless you tell me to, I'm not stopping at one kiss. Not this time."

His words turned up the heat enveloping Robin like the flame on a gas grill. "Let's go to my place," she said, slipping her arms around his neck and tipping back her head.

Charlie scooped her into his arms, showing her that his shoulder was completely healed. "My place is closer."

Robin laughed delightedly as he carried her past his astonished guests and headed straight for the exit.

Once Charlie managed to set her into the passenger side of his pick up without dropping her, they didn't speak again until he pulled up in front of his luxury apartment.

"If you weren't the sheriff, you might have gotten a speeding ticket," she pointed out with a smirk as he shut off the engine.

He looked at her with eyes that were dark with passion. "I'll turn myself in on Monday," he growled. "No, better make that a week from Monday."

By the time his meaning dawned on her, he'd gotten out of the truck and come around to her side. When he opened her door and extended his hand, she peeked up at him through her lashes. Mascara made them feel sinfully thick when she fluttered them.

"A week might be long enough," she purred, empowered by his obvious attraction to her.

Color washed over his cheekbones, and he wrapped his hand around the back of her neck. "I can't think straight when I'm around you." He tipped back her head and feasted on her mouth.

It was just the reaction Robin had been hoping for when she'd bought the red dress. She barely even noticed when someone driving by wolf-whistled shrilly, but Charlie broke off the kiss and swore under his breath.

''Come inside,'' he whispered.

Easygoing Charlie, her best buddy, had been replaced by a passionate male whose every glance, every touch, swept aside her worries about pleasing him. She had no qualms about giving herself freely, fully, because she knew that deep inside, this sensual stranger was the man she loved. He wouldn't hurt her.

Charlie only dropped his keys once, swearing colorfully as he fumbled with his front door. The little sign that he, too, was nervous, was the last bit of reassurance she needed.

Once he'd gotten the door open, he surprised her by taking her hands in his.

''Are you sure?'' he asked. ''When I saw that dress, the whole package…did I leap to the wrong conclusion just because that was what I wanted so badly to see tonight? If this isn't what you want—'' he swallowed hard ''—we'll take a step back.''

She could see what the offer had cost him. Her heart, already so full of love for him, expanded even more.

''I'm sure,'' she said softly.

Once they entered his apartment, he surprised her by not pouncing on her and not ripping off her clothes. Instead he nibbled, he tasted, he praised her. He unwrapped her like the best gift he'd ever received. They left a trail of clothing from the living room to the bedroom.

Finally they ended up at the side of Charlie's massive king-size bed. Wearing her aunt's garnet earrings and a scrap of red lace, Robin watched him strip away his briefs. He was everything she had imagined, even better.

"You're beautiful," she breathed, skating her hand down the center of his chest. His muscles quivered beneath her fingertips.

"Thank you for entrusting yourself to me," he replied. He ran his hands lovingly over her sensitized skin, cupping her breasts, stroking her hips, until her legs were too weak to hold her.

He did his best to be gentle, to lead her slowly along passion's path, but Robin had other ideas. She approached his control like a chess game, one strategic move at a time. They circled, they stalked, and ultimately, as in all the best games, they both won.

Afterward he cuddled her close, as though he couldn't bear to let her go. She lay in the circle of his arm, her body draped bonelessly over his.

"My word," she murmured, smiling against his chest as her pulse and her breathing slowly returned to normal.

"That's just what I was thinking," he said as he stroked his free hand down her arm. "Oh, my word."

Robin must have dozed off, because when she opened her eyes, Charlie had propped himself up against the pillows, and the sheet had slid down to his waist.

Robin scrambled to a sitting position. What was the protocol here? Did she dress while he watched, a striptease in reverse? Was a shower allowed before she left?

She turned to ask, but he was watching her so intently that the words died on her tongue.

"What is it?" she whispered instead.

"Did you wonder why I changed the name of my club from Charlie's Heart to Charlie's?" he asked.

His question threw her off. "Um, because you wanted a new sign?" she guessed helplessly. Pillow talk, that must be what this was.

"Let me tell you a little story." He took her hand, stroking the back of it with his thumb. "When I sold my share of the ranch to Adam and Travis, I was looking for something, but I wasn't sure what. I opened the club and it became important to me. It made me happy." He curved his mouth into a smile, but his eyes remained serious. "I guess you could say it had my heart." He cleared his throat. "But not anymore."

Robin began to tremble. Her chest felt tight. Her entire body tingled with hope, with expectation.

"I love you," he said softly. "I haven't said that to a girl since seventh grade. I'm sure I meant it then, and I sure as heaven mean it now."

Tears of happiness blurred his image until Robin blinked them away. "I love you, too," she said, cupping her hand against his cheek. "My friend, my lover. You make me so happy. You give me so much."

He turned away for a moment, reaching for something on the nightstand that she hadn't noticed before. A ring box.

Astonishment swept through her as she watched him open it, revealing a glittering ring.

"I hadn't planned to propose in bed," he said, his voice rough. "I bought it a week after you came to Waterloo, and it's been waiting for you to claim it ever since."

As he took the ring from the box, she noticed the shape of the center diamond. "It's breathtaking," she murmured.

"That's why I had to change the name of my club," he replied, "because, corny as it sounds, Charlie's heart belongs to you now, if you want it."

"Oh, yes," Robin sobbed, holding out a hand that shook so badly he had to steady it while he slid the ring on her finger. "I want your heart and the rest of you, too."

When he kissed her, she realized that Charlie's heart, and his love, were now hers to keep. Just as her heart belonged to him, and always would.

* * * * *

Look for David and Kim's story,
coming in 2003 from Silhouette Special Edition.

COMING NEXT MONTH

SPECIAL EDITION

#1519 HER HEALING TOUCH—Lindsay McKenna
Morgan's Mercenaries: Destiny's Women

Angel Paredes, a paramedic in the Peruvian Army, was known for her legendary powers of healing but could not heal her own wounded heart. When she was paired with handsome Special Forces Officer Burke Gifford for a life-threatening mission, she discovered love was the true healer, and that Burke was the only one who could save her....

#1520 COMPLETELY SMITTEN—Susan Mallery
Hometown Heartbreakers

When preacher's daughter and chronic good-girl Haley Foster was all but dumped by her fiancé, she took off on a road trip, determined to change her people-pleasing ways. Kevin Harmon, a reformed bad boy and U.S. Marshal wound up right in the middle of Haley's plans. Was it possible that these two opposites could end up completely smitten?

#1521 A FATHER'S FORTUNE—Shirley Hailstock

Erin Taylor loved children, but she'd long ago given up on having a family of her own—until she hired James "Digger" Clayton to renovate her day-care center. One smile at a time, this brawny builder was reshaping her heart.... Could she convince him to try his hand at happily-ever-after?

#1522 THERE GOES THE BRIDE—Crystal Green
Kane's Crossing

When full-figured ex-beauty queen Daisy Cox left her cheating groom at the altar, Rick Shane piloted her to safety. The love-wary ex-soldier only planned to rescue a damsel-in-distress, never realizing that he might fall for this runaway bride!

#1523 WEDDING OF THE CENTURY—Patricia McLinn

You could say Annette Trevetti and Steve Corbett had a history together. Seven years ago, their wedding was interrupted by Steve's ex-girlfriend—carrying a baby she claimed was his! Annette left town promptly, then returned years later to find Steve a single father to another man's child. Was their love strong enough to overcome their past misunderstanding?

#1524 FAMILY MERGER—Leigh Greenwood

Ron Egan was a high-powered businessman who learned that no amount of money could solve all his problems. For suddenly his sixteen-year-old daughter was pregnant, and in a home for unwed mothers. Kathryn Roper, who ran the home, agreed to help Ron reconnect with his daughter—and maybe make a connection of their own....